Early praise for On The Edge

"*On the Edge* is quite the ride. Buckman and his team take on Red and Reacher. It is a fast paced read, kept me on the edge of my seat from beginning to end. Can't wait for the next one."

—Gary Banter

"I couldn't turn the pages fast enough. Reed has a gift for making her written words come to life. And the details are impeccable. Reed and Hawkins make a great team."

—Kayla Price

"A very real and relevant story. Makes you think about what's going on around you. Hawkins has clearly been around the block. Reed keeps you hooked to the very last page. An awesome read."

—Keegan Reed

"Move over Reacher, there's a new kid in town. Buckman is a true crime fiction hero, surrounded by a team of experts in their field. They'll make you laugh, make you cry and keep you on the edge of your seat. Together they take on the world of corruption with a bang. They are colourful, vibrant characters entangled in international intrigue. You won't want to put this book down."

— P.L. Stokes

ON THE EDGE

A COLE BUCKMAN NOVEL

Written by Marina L. Reed

Story by Don Hawkins

First Printing: 2022
CHICKEN HOUSE PRESS

Library and Archives Canada Cataloguing in Publication
CIP data on file with the National Library and Archives

ISBN trade paperback edition: 978-1-990336-20-1

Chicken House Press
282906 Normanby/Bentinck Townline
Durham, Ontario, Canada, N0G 1R0

www.chickenhousepress.ca

Cover art by J. Mitchel Reed

Other Books by Marina L. Reed

<u>Fiction</u>
Primrose Street
It's Lonely in Paradise
Love Lies Bleeding

Coming soon...
A Cole Buckman Novel: Shadow Man.

<u>Non-Fiction</u>
A new paradigm for grief series
  Remember, It's OK: Loss of a Parent
  Remember, It's OK: Loss of a Partner
  Remember, It's OK: Loss of a Sibling/Friend
  Remember, It's OK: Loss of a Child
  Remember, It's OK: Loss of a Pet
  Remember, It's OK: Loss for Teens
Jayne's INpowered Handbook

Visit **MarinaLReed.com** to learn more, order her books, and access free PDFs.

ON THE EDGE

Marina L. Reed
Story by Don Hawkins

CHAPTER ONE

THURSDAY, MAY 7 | LATE AFTERNOON | CANADA | 2015

Cole Buckman, a.k.a. Boss, leaned over the railing on the second floor overlooking the luxurious lobby of Toronto's elite hotel, the Royal York. Comfortable chairs were presented in small clusters, allowing for private conversations. Long, multilayered chandeliers hung from the warm, wood-panelled ceiling, creating an elegant atmosphere. A large clock at the far end of the gallery kept an eye on the proceedings, methodically ticking the seconds into minutes. The second-floor balcony wrapped around the lobby, a perfect vantage point. Dignitaries and world leaders in suits or silk dresses sat in chair clusters or milled about, sipping tall flutes of Champagne or Perrier. Serving staff invisibly wove their way around the suits and dresses, wearing all black with white linen napkins folded over their forearms, looking for empty glasses to refill. Rehearsed laughter and stilted tones wafted up, settling around Cole's feet. He liked it that way. Knowing someone's discomfort. Someone's weakness. It gave him the edge to always be one step ahead.

The British prime minister talked with the foreign minister from Japan. Even from a distance, Buckman could see the conversation was strained. That was his job. To notice everything. He was the MI6 agent responsible for the life of the British prime minister. And he was the best there was, which explained why the PM always asked for him personally.

The prime minister's bodyguard stood a few feet away, subtly watching the Japanese minister and others moving in the room. Each dignitary had their own bodyguard. On top of that, there were security officers from each country, all wearing dark business suits with white shirts and ties, white open-collar shirts for the female officers. If that wasn't enough protection, the Royal Canadian Mounted Police (RCMP) added four of their own officers for each dignitary, wearing the same dark suit and each sporting a Smith & Wesson 5946, complete with the unique horse design on its grip, in their belt holster. Visiting security personnel could be carrying Glocks or HKs, but only if the RCMP had given approval.

A lot of power stood hip-to-hip in that room. Palpable tension. Everyone looked for a problem. It wasn't a friendly afternoon in the sandbox, and most didn't play nice. The police manning the doors were in standard Toronto Police Department uniforms. Other than the white napkin over the arm, to the untrained eye it would be difficult to pick out who was a dignitary, a server, a bodyguard, or security officer. Everyone dressed the same, which was probably the point. Buckman watched as bodyguards lifted wrist to mouth, sending a code or a warning through their private, secure radio channel. The bodyguards were all wirelessly connected. If luminous, the colliding frequencies in the room would have resembled an intricate laser-beam web. Buckman picked out the security pins on protective details, one of the few ways to distinguish one from the other. He saw movement at the right and left of his peripheral vision. The uniformed police officers were moving in to lock the double doors at the far end of the gallery, leading into a large conference room. The Environmental Summit was about to begin.

As Buckman scanned the room from the balcony, he slowed every movement down, eliminated extraneous noise, and zoomed in his focus. He looked for anything out of place: an untied shoelace, a waiter's napkin on the incorrect arm, a sideways glance, a hand in a pocket. The focus had been Champagne and idle chatter. Now there was a shift. Shifts could be trouble. Shifts asked for trouble, invited it. Buckman adjusted the knot of his tie, moving his head slightly as he settled it into place, then slid his hand down its length. He closed one button on his dark, finely woven wool jacket. Automatically, his hand did a comfort slide over his P7 Heckler & Koch semiautomatic nestled in the holster inside his jacket. It was still his gun of choice, small, easy to hide if necessary, eight rounds in a clip, quick draw, ready to fire. It had saved his ass more times than he cared to remember. For extra insurance, he always strapped his Fairbairn-Sykes fighting knife along the lower, outside part of his calf. His grandfather had given it to him when he started middle school and had told him it was his secret weapon during the war. He called it his stiletto of luck. Buckman had carried the knife through high school, learning how to handle it so he wouldn't fall victim to the resident hall bullies.

As a young boy, Cole was small and scrawny, a perfect target for a school bully. He learned the art of stealth early. For survival, he learned to read and respond to a situation before it could unravel—often before it could even begin. He discovered he could alter a scene, slow things down, assess movements and intentions. He didn't have to see a situation with his eyes—he could sense activity. He remembered a time at the beginning of middle school. Cole was facing his locker, trying to get the combination of his lock to work. The back of his neck felt chilly, and he slowed things down. He paid attention. He could tell that Jeff, a kid that had bullied him as far back as second grade, was walking toward him. Cole's peripheral vision told him Jeff's fist was clenched, there was a hungry scowl on his face, and his foot slid out, ready to trip Cole when he stepped back. But Cole was ready. He stepped back, but instead of tripping and falling over Jeff's foot and getting punched in the face, he sidestepped it in a dancelike movement, fluidly drawing his knife, bending down like he was falling, nicking Jeff's ankle enough to draw a speck of blood and cause pain. Cole quickly holstered his knife, rolled on the floor as if he had fallen, got up, brushed off his pants, and without even glancing at Jeff, walked to class. Things changed after that. He never got bullied again. The knife had become like an appendage. It had become his 'stiletto of good luck.'

Buckman felt that familiar chill on the back of his neck. It was his radar. It always happened when things were quiet, just before the Jack jumped out of the box.

He knew all the doors in the building were guarded, especially the conference room where the meetings were being held. But there were so many ways in and out. He knew the hotel well. And then he saw it out of the corner of his eye, like burst shots from a camera on continuous high speed: a waiter reaching into his pocket, the napkin slipping from his arm, the British prime minister moving out of his sightline as he neared the conference room doors. Buckman dashed to the stairs. He calculated the seconds it would take for him to reach the first floor. He picked up rapid movement to his right, someone heading for the elevators. Buckman turned and raced in that direction. The waiter glanced over his shoulder while pushing the elevator button repeatedly. The doors opened. He stepped inside and turned to face the front, watching

Cole's approach as the doors began to close. He smiled a thin smile. Buckman pushed off with his right foot and caught the edge of the door with his fingers, enough to stop the mechanism from closing. He pulled himself up and stepped into the elevator. The doors closed behind him.

He didn't need to catch his breath. He wiggled the knot of his tie back into place and buttoned his jacket. The muscles under his shirt rippled with anticipation. He waited. Kept cool. Waited. It was what kept his scores low on the golf course. It was what kept him alive in the field. He took one step closer to the waiter, who was breathing quickly. Sweating. Reaching his right hand slowly into his pocket.

Buckman nodded toward the guy's jacket. "What's in there?" *He's clearly not a waiter*, he thought, and the guy's left hand flew forward toward Cole's face. Buckman lifted his arm to block, but the guy was good. Clearly not his first tussle. He went for Cole's ribcage, ripping the button off his jacket. Buckman liked a challenge, but he didn't like it when someone messed with his suit. He saw the guy's right hand pull a Glock 27 out of his pocket. Buckman moved his head forward, fast, colliding with the bridge of the guy's nose, breaking it in spectacular fashion, sending blood splattering onto the poster on the back panel of the elevator advertising fine dining in the restaurant downstairs. Buckman sank his fist into the guy's solar plexus, pushing up toward his ribs. As he curled over, Buckman lifted his knee directly into the man's chin, sending one of his teeth into the corner of the elevator. More blood. The guy slumped to the floor.

Buckman reached into his pocket, pulled out his cell, and pushed a number. "Immediate assistance. Area 2." He pushed B1 on the elevator panel. He wedged the Glock 27 back into the guy's pocket. When the doors opened, three police officers were standing, waiting. Buckman dragged the guy out by his jacket collar and dropped him at the police officers' feet. "Code T, Tom," was all he said as he turned back into the elevator and pushed *Lobby*.

The police officers handcuffed Cole's delivery, and confiscated his weapon. They read him his Miranda rights, Canadian-style, while putting him in the back of their cruiser. The car wove its way through the maze of the underground parking lot and finally exited onto the city streets, where they battled traffic, construction, streetcars, buses, and pedestrians until arriving at the local police division's cell block. They stopped at the gatepost intercom for entry and parked outside. Both officers escorted their new friend inside, one on either side.

The booking area was a large, open room with benches in front of steel loops secured into the wall. Three other visitors were shackled there, waiting. The officers paraded their companion in front of the cell sergeant, confirming his arrest. The suspect continued to be silent, not asking for a lawyer, not giving his name. They made notes of his injuries, visibly a broken nose, possibly cheekbone, possible broken rib, and bruising. They took him to a private search room. All clothing and shoes were taken. A note was made about a tattoo on the back of his left shoulder, small but distinct, a red round table with a black sword through the centre, blade pointing up, not down. He was given a white Tyvek suit to wear, a crappy sandwich, and was put in a cell with a concrete bench, a steel toilet, and sink for the night.

THURSDAY, MAY 7 | LATE EVENING | ITALY

"What the hell was he doing there? How did he get caught? Fuck. This is just unacceptable. He has too much information."

He hung up, snapped the phone in half, and threw it across the room. He walked over to his decanter and poured himself a drink. He must have found out. But how?

He walked over to his desk, shot back the contents in his glass, placed it on the table, and picked up a second phone. He dialled a number and it rang exactly three times. There was breathing on the other end. He didn't wait for a voice. "Covert Cell; Code Red. Details and location to follow." He hung up and went to pour another drink before using a third phone that would provide the details for the hit he just ordered.

FRIDAY, MAY 8 | MORNING | CANADA

Buckman unlocked the door to his rented condo after finishing a long run. He was used to the rental world. He had never really lived in one place. That was his life, always on the move. And his rentals or hotel rooms were more than adequate. He travelled light: a gym bag and a shoulder satchel. The satchel kept his documents, his technology, a small knight figurine his mother had given him when he entered the Academy, and a tiny metal model airplane from Mac.

It was a cool, crisp morning. The sun flirted with the clouds, threatening to melt the last few piles of dirt-speckled leftover spring snow. He felt good but wanted a steaming hot shower and then breakfast. He had found a little place down the road the other day. Superb coffee. Great home fries. He dropped his running shoes by the door and walked down the hall to the bathroom. His phone on the kitchen counter began to vibrate. He rarely had it on ring. He hated the noise. He walked over, pushed the speaker icon, and poured himself a glass of water. Bob Newgate's name popped onto his screen.

"Cole, how are you? Getting you at a bad time?"

"Being on the phone is always a bad time. Whatta you need, Bob?"

"Well, a couple of tournaments are coming up, and we

wondered if you wanted to extend your contract for another year."

"TaylorMade can't live without me. Well, I do still love that new driver. Do I get a new set of clubs out of the deal this time?"

"You always want a little more, Buckman."

"Of course I do, that's why you love me." They both chuckled. Buckman chugged his glass of water.

"See you at the tournament next week then?"

"Is there any other place I'd rather be?"

"Not from where I'm standing. We'll look after the paperwork then. Sound good?"

"Sounds good. Take care, Bob. See you in the winner's circle."

"I'm counting on it."

Buckman hung up and headed for the shower. He could almost taste those golden, crunchy home fries.

While Buckman turned on the water, the prisoner transports began arriving from local police stations, parking on the back street outside the Toronto courthouse. Once inside, the passengers had their shackles and handcuffs removed and were herded down a corridor to the holding pen. There was a large orange sports cooler where Tang was dispensed in cone-shaped paper cups, and options of meat or vegetarian sandwiches were on the menu. The holding pen was filling up with various charges: criminal, mental, domestic abuse, drunk driving. A regular morning-after party. Some were passed out on the floor, other were pacing, standing, or sitting on the bench. There was one toilet in the corner, only for pissing. Soon the big boys and girls would come to join the party, the ones in the orange jumpsuits with blue slipcovers on their canvas shoes, from the big detention centres. There was lots of noise as prisoners were called for their hearing or to speak with their counsel through Plexiglas, or just because they were ranting or banging bars.

The guy with the tattoo behind his left shoulder stood quietly in the back corner, his thumbs looped into the waistband of his pants. Nothing moved except his eyes as they surveyed the room inside and out. The morning became midmorning, became late morning.

"John Doe?" an officer yelled into the bullpen. The man with the tattoo slowly made his way to the gate, stepping over bodies, jostling others with his shoulders. He was handcuffed and marched down the corridor to face his bail hearing.

Cole quietly opened the heavy oak doors and slipped into the courtroom in Old City Hall, already in session. He discreetly arranged himself into a seat at the back since most of the gallery was full. The air was thick and stale and smelled of photocopied paper, unwashed bodies, and Chanel. It was not a place for a picnic. Clearly a busy day in the world of bail hearings.

As an MI6 agent, Buckman was kept busy travelling around the world. His cover as a professional golf pro made it easy to slip in and out of cities and across borders. It also meant that he was rarely in his country of birth, Canada, and hardly ever in Toronto, where his father lived and worked, unless he was playing at a tournament, on assignment, or protecting the British prime minister. So, he wasn't going to miss this opportunity to see his dad in action. After his mom died shortly after his twenty-fifth birthday, his dad had thrown himself into his work. It had been almost fifteen years, but sometimes Buckman felt like he lost his dad a bit that day too.

It was a relatively small room, seating a maximum of about fifty people of all races and demographics. Railings separated the audience from the players: judge, defence, accused, prosecutor, police officers, clerks. Kitch Buckman had been brought in for this case. He had become rather famous in the last number of years for putting away slippery criminals. The accused had been coy and crafty, not offering any statement, fingerprints not to be found in the system. The gun in his pocket was the golden ticket that at least allowed them to arrest the guy. Clerks sat in front of the judge in their small booths, typing continuously. Their constant clicking on keys fell into rhythm with the irritating drone of the air conditioner.

Old buildings, old technology.

The accused sat handcuffed in his cubicle at the left side of the courtroom. He still wore the white painter's outfit, his face expressionless. His defence attorney was a young woman. Her light blue headscarf accentuated her strong bone structure and piercing dark eyes. She wore a dark blue pantsuit and high-heeled shoes. Buckman could see her intense focus.

Kitch Buckman sat at the desk across the aisle, adjacent to the defence attorney, shuffling papers around. He was still handsome. His dark brown hair was beginning to grey around the temples, but he was fit, strong. His pinstripe suit moulded around his 5'10" frame. His rectangular, dark-framed glasses magnified his clear blue eyes, exactly the same as Cole's. Except for the grey at the temples and the age difference, they could have been brothers. Kitch pushed his chair back, stood, and addressed the Justice of the Peace.

"Your Worship, for the record, my name is Buckman, Kitch Buckman, special prosecutor assigned to this particular case. As we have not been provided with a name for the accused at this time, he will be referred to as John Doe. Unless, of course, my esteemed colleague can provide us with a name." Kitch looked over to the defence council. He hesitated briefly, his forehead creasing as his eyes focused on the face of the accused. He blinked quickly, regaining composure, and sat back down.

His reaction had been minimal. He was sure no one had noticed. His recovery had been swift. *What the hell is he doing here?* thought Kitch. *Why is he not giving his name? Something has gone terribly wrong. I'll have to play along until I can get to him myself. What the fuck?*

The defence council stood and meekly addressed the bench. "Your Worship, for the record, my name is Fatima Sundra. I have been appointed duty counsel for the gentlemen before the court. At this time, we are unable to provide his name. However, he does have the right to silence and is protected under the common law confessions rule, and section 7 and section 11(c) of the Canadian Charter of Rights and Freedoms." She sat down, trying to hide her embarrassed frustration.

It was 11:45 a.m. The Justice of the Peace was clearly irritated by the uncooperative behaviour of the accused. She was also not impressed with being read chapter and verse about the law from a new lawyer in her court. She clenched her jaw, glaring over the top of her spectacles at the counsel, and then took a sip of water. It had been a long morning. It looked to be a long afternoon, and she wanted her lunch break. She ordered the accused to stand. No response. She did so again. No response. The Justice glanced over at two police officers who approached the prisoner box, telling him to stand as he had been asked.

Nothing. An oppressive cloud hovered in the courtroom. Everyone spoke with their eyes looking from one to another, from the Justice to the accused, from lawyer to lawyer. Kitch stood, breaking the spell.

"If it please Your Worship. John Doe is charged with being in possession of an unregistered restricted weapon, a Glock 27 handgun. He was trespassing at an international political event at the Royal York Hotel yesterday, where world leaders were in attendance. On behalf of the Crown, we are requesting the accused not be granted bail and be held in custody at this time. We currently have no assurance that he would return for future court appearances." Kitch sat down and pulled his papers into a neat pile in front of him. He felt an uncharacteristic bead of sweat under his collar.

"May I suggest," said Fatima, rising to her feet, "we return to court in two days. I will work with my client to produce the needed information."

"Your Worship, the Crown will need at least three days to allow for a police investigation."

"Accused is to be held for three days," announced the JOP. "Bail is denied."

"Permission to leave court, Your Worship?" said Kitch, since he was only present for that one particular case that day.

"Permission granted," said the JOP. "Good to see you, Mr. Buckman."

Kitch smiled and nodded respectfully in response. He put his papers into his briefcase, locked it closed, and stood up. Everyone was leaving for lunch. He tried to get the attention of the accused but he was talking with his lawyer and there were too many people. As he looked toward the back doors, a pair of blue eyes caught his attention. His face opened into a full grin, and he waved. Cole waved back. As he walked to the rear of the courtroom, he noticed the accused being escorted through the side door near the front. His window was closing. He took a deep breath and focused on his son.

They greeted each other in a bear hug. Kitch took his son by the shoulders and held him at arms' length. "My god, it's good to see you, boy. It has been a while."

"Too long, Dad."

"What are you doing here? I had no idea you were coming. Why didn't you let me know?"

"You know the drill, security, security, security. When I heard there was going to be a bail hearing, I took my chances that you would be working."

"Well, I'm glad you did. I'm very glad you did. Are you flying out this afternoon, or do you have time to grab lunch and maybe a pint?"

"I'd love to have lunch."

"Great. I just have to tie up a few ends. Will only take a couple minutes. Go out front and meet me around the side entrance. You know the door?"

"I do. The paddy wagon express lane."

Kitch laughed. "Haven't heard that for a while. Very good. Yes, that's the spot. I want to hear what you've been up to."

"Why not just head out the front doors with me now?"

"Just have to make sure a few things are taken care of before I leave. Won't take a minute. We'll grab a cab out back. See you there in five?"

"See you in five."

Kitch put his hand on Cole's arm and gave it a squeeze, then turned and walked back through the courtroom and out the prisoner's exit, his heart pounding. He put his finger underneath his collar, pulling it out for more air.

When he got to the holding area, he asked for John Doe and was told he had already been taken for transportation back to the police cells. Kitch turned and walked down the stark, bare hall toward the door. John Doe was being led by two police officers about twenty metres ahead. Kitch picked up his pace, hoping to catch them, his arm in front to stop the door from closing as he followed them out onto the street, close at their heels.

The prisoner van stood waiting while John Doe approached. Kitch called out. The prisoner turned. Then, like the Jiffy Pop tin foil puffing into a dome of heat, there was a flurry of pops. Within seconds, both officers were on the ground, John Doe had bullets in his body, and Kitch had taken a stray bullet spray.

Hearing the noise, Cole came around the corner at a run and made a quick assessment of the situation. He ran to his dad on the ground, pressing his hands over his wound, blood seeping through his fingers. Sirens were already screaming at close range.

———————

The doors to the emergency room crashed open as paramedics wheeled Kitch in on a stretcher. Cole came in behind and was directed to the nurse's station to fill out the paperwork while they took Kitch to a curtained cubicle to stabilize him and prep him for immediate surgery. The smell of sanitizer and old paint hovered in the emergency room while machines beeped and patients moaned and sighed or cried. It wasn't as if it was Cole's first time in an emergency room. He had suffered his fair share of wounds or had to bring those in who had suffered wounds inflicted by him. But this was different. This was his own father.

There were eight areas sectioned off by thin, light blue curtains. Kitch lay in the middle one. Under the curtain, Cole could see pairs of Nike shoes moving around each other, hems of blue and green scrub pants bouncing on the laces and swinging around ankles, punctuated by wheels of hospital equipment moving in and out. It was like watching a dance recital.

He turned back to the documents. Picked up a pen to sign, then moved to his dad's cubicle. He pulled back the curtain.

Three medics worked on his dad. He stood back while they put tubes up his nose, stuck patches onto his chest, disinfected the bullet wounds, and inserted needles into his arms that were attached to intravenous poles. When two of the attendants stepped away, Cole moved in.

His dad was still conscious but getting groggier by the second because of the sedation for surgery. Kitch grabbed Cole's hand. His grip was firm. Cole leaned his ear down, close to his lips.

"You playing any golf?"

Cole stared at his dad. Then he smiled. "Of course, tournament next week."

"Well, what are you still doing here? Come back with some good news for me. And find out who did this."

"I'll do both." Cole squeezed his hand. Kitch's eyes slowly closed, and they wheeled him down the hall and through a double off-limits door.

When Cole was too young to hold a gun, his dad put a golf club in his hand instead. They played together often, and Cole got good. Really good. Good enough to go pro.

When he got older, he and his dad would flip: gun range or golf course for a Saturday afternoon. Cole had become proficient with both guns and clubs. Both ended up serving his profession later on.

"We'll call you when he's out of surgery, Mr. Buckman," a nurse said.

"Thank you." Cole stood looking at the closed doors, knowing his dad was on the other side, fighting for his life. He'd always been a fighter. He started out on the police force near Windsor, Ontario. Cole grew up hearing stories that often were the things nightmares were made of. But his dad always came home. Always. He would hear him come into the pitch-black house late at night as he lay awake, waiting to hear the front door close quietly. Then there would be the sound of his dad putting his gun in the cabinet, his coat on the chair. Sometimes he'd go into the kitchen and grab a beer and some chips and sit down in front of the television. Other times he'd just come right upstairs, the steps creaking in all the weak places, the hall boards groaning under his weight. He'd hear his mother whispering, softly crying, and his dad comforting her. It wouldn't be until the next day that Cole would hear the story or see the new bandage. It was his dad's new partner, Paul, that told him the story one time. How they were called out to a shooting at a farmhouse late at night. How Kitch had said they would be the SWAT team because they were ten minutes out. How Kitch organized the fire department and other police officers in the takedown. How Kitch walked into the farmhouse cool as a cucumber, and next thing everyone knew, he was walking out with the guy in handcuffs. There was a nick out of his jacket, and blood had been dripping down his arm. But it was all over. Paul called it Kitch's law: fire second, talk first. Cole remembered thinking how Paul had probably watered down the story for him. Cole always worried that one time, "Kitch's law" might get him killed.

Cole was relieved when his dad decided to leave the force and become a lawyer. He had told Cole he wanted to fry bigger fish. Cole never really knew what that meant until he joined the force himself. He wanted to be like his dad, so really, it was all Kitch's fault. Soon he was sending his dad the "bigger fish." His dad had taught him to be a fighter. He'd learned from the best. He'd be back. Cole knew he would be.

Right now, Cole had work to do. He turned from the closed double doors, took a deep breath, and walked down the cold, white hall, through the revolving doors, and onto the street. He hailed a cab.

"500 Lake Shore Boulevard West," Cole told the driver.

FRIDAY, MAY 8 | LATE AFTERNOON | CANADA

A white GMC traders panel van with a small ladder on the roof and HVAC company name written on the side careened into the Holiday Inn parking lot on the outskirts of Toronto. It pulled into a spot beside a grey Ford Explorer; rust around the wheel rims, floater crack on the windshield. There were few cars in the lot, not a soul to be seen. A muscular man exited the white van dressed in a dark blue pair of coveralls, a name badge stitched over his left breast pocket, Harmon, the name of the company stitched over the right. Three other people stepped out behind him, all wearing the same coveralls: a small woman, a tall man, and a muscular woman. No one was smiling. No one spoke. They had been brought together by the Strike Force: mercenaries for hire. They only knew each other by their handles and expertise.

They got to work changing license plates and peeling the company name off the white van. The coveralls were shoved into garbage bags. They wore jeans and grey t-shirts underneath, except for Cobra, who always wore the same shirt for a mission.

"Fuck," said Cobra. "I've lost a button."

"Search through the bullet casings as we put them into the garbage bag. Hopefully it's there," said Berea.

"Or under one of the seats," suggested DangPa.

"What a fucking train wreck," said Cobra.

"Easy. It's one goddamn button," said Berea.

"Exactly," she said, frothing fury.

"Why weren't your coveralls zipped up?" asked Dagger.

Cobra gave him a white-hot glare. The conversation was over.

They cleaned out the van, wiping it down for fingerprints inside and out.

"There's no button," said Dagger.

"Maybe it was missing before we started," said DangPa.

"I would have noticed. I never miss details," said Cobra.

Berea took the garbage bags over to the green dumpster positioned behind the vans. They each grabbed their weapons from the vehicle, locked it, tossed the keys behind the dumpster, and climbed into the Ford Explorer.

"One of us needs to report in," said Berea.

Dagger opened his burner phone and made the call.

DangPa put on her sunglasses as Berea drove out of the parking lot. They were headed to a hotel near Pearson International Airport.

FRIDAY, MAY 8 | EUROPE

While Buckman made his way back to his rented condo in Toronto, a heavyset man listened intently as he was briefed about an incident that occurred there. He had a tattoo of a red round table and a sword pointing up through the centre on the back of his left shoulder.

"What the hell was he doing there?" he asked between clenched teeth, stained yellow from too much tobacco. "We all could have been exposed. Was he eliminated?"

"Yes, just as you ordered."

"Did he talk to anyone?"

"We don't think so."

"Who apprehended him?"

"We aren't sure. A professional. Happened very quickly."

The large man tapped his unlit cigar impatiently on the top of his desk. "There was a complication?"

"Yes. Kitch Buckman."

"Kitch Buckman?" He stopped tapping and looked directly at the man answering his questions. He was clearly shocked.

"Yes."

"Why was he there?"

"I am unaware of that piece of information."

"Are you aware of where he is at the moment?"

"Hospital. Surgery."

"So he is still alive."

"He is."

The large man turned and picked up the CZ 75 from his desk, stroking it like he was shining a Christmas ornament.

"Find out why he was there at that exact moment."

"Of course."

The heavy man turned away, putting the gun back down on his desk and lighting the cigar. He inhaled deeply then puffed some clouds of smoke lovingly into the air as he spoke. "That's all."

He waited until he heard the door close. He picked up his phone.

SATURDAY, MAY 9 | AFTERNOON | CANADA

Kitch Buckman came through the surgery well. Cole stood at the end of his bed. He watched him sleep amidst the lullaby of beeping machines keeping him alive. A nurse came into the room and told Cole his father would stay in the ICU for a few more days so he could be monitored carefully. It was not the first time Cole had visited his dad in an ICU accommodation. The first time was when he was still a police officer and had been shot on duty. That was a close call. The second had been in Ireland. That had been after he left the police force and had gone to get his law degree. He started as assistant crown attorney and soon found himself on special assignment to deal with IRA members working in Ontario. But one investigation had taken him into the belly of the beast: Ireland herself. He had become a trusted advisor on high-level projects, made inroads with the international intelligence community, and ended up in an Irish ICU because of a bullet that narrowly missed his heart. His dad always seemed to know how to dodge a bullet. Cole smiled to himself as he walked down the hospital corridor to the elevator. In many ways, he had followed in his father's footsteps, just not into an ICU—yet.

He was lost in thought as the hospital's elevator doors opened and a man in an expensive suit walked out as Cole stepped inside. The man was tense, agitated. Cole put it down to the fact that it was a hospital and everyone was agitated. Cole was agitated about one thing: why had there been a shooting behind the courthouse at all?

While Buckman visited his dad in the hospital, the Cell had checked out of their hotel rooms, changed their hair colour and clothes, ditched the grey Ford Explorer, and were on their way by taxi to a private plane waiting for them on the runway.

They were mercenaries for hire from countries around the world, all highly trained and bringing a lethal combination of skills: British SAS computer genius gone rogue, Korean contract explosive expert, American defected FBI agent, Canadian ex-special forces sniper with a bone to pick. They had all worked solo until recently, when they had been brought together. The driving force behind their choices was money and adrenaline.

They slung their weapons of choice over their shoulders as they walked to board the Strike Force's private Gulfstream g550. To a bystander, it looked like they were carrying large musical instruments over their shoulders or pulling them behind. Their weapons were cleverly concealed in and around the instruments inside the cases.

Cobra didn't go anywhere without her FNAB-43

weapon. It was part of her body. Everyone else stowed their gear at the back of the cabin; Cobra kept hers in the seat beside her.

They buckled in and enjoyed a drink, knowing they had a lot of work to do in six and a half hours when the wheels touched down in Las Vegas. They had two weeks before the big fight was scheduled.

SUNDAY, MAY 10 | AFTERNOON | USA

Kitch had been dozing when Cole stopped by the hospital one last time before catching his flight. He had seen his dad more in the last three days than he had in the last three years. He felt relaxed sitting in his window seat on the Airbus, knowing his father was recovering well in the ICU.

Buckman stepped out of the airplane into the warm, thick air of the southern United States. He quickly cleared customs and folded himself into the back of the limo waiting for him outside the airport. His golf clubs and attire were neatly packed into the trunk. A coffee and cruller donut were waiting for him. His favourite. Bob thought of everything.

"Good afternoon, Mr. Buckman. To the hotel first, sir?"

"No, let's get right to the course. I'll change there. Give me a chance to see who I'm up against. Swing a few clubs. Gets me loosened up before an event starts."

"Very good, sir."

Buckman leaned back, savouring his coffee and cruller. He had sported more guns in his hands in the last few weeks than golf clubs. He knew he would have to play at least moderately well to maintain his place on the tour and keep his cover secure. He always seemed to find his swing quickly in the past. Like riding a bike. He hoped this tournament would be no different. He knew the course well, having played it many times. The fifteenth hole had always been his nemesis. He would make sure to practice some new strategy for success this time. He needed to practice, but he also had to see if there was a caddy he could hire. He couldn't risk having the same caddy each tournament. He made up a story about keeping his game fresh, which was why he liked switching his caddy. Whether other players believed him or not, people had given up asking.

He couldn't stop thinking about who and why there had been a shooting after the bail hearing last Friday. Who was that John Doe? He wished he could have just started the search for the shooter the next day, but he had to play this tournament. He hoped it would clear his head, allow him to strategize, know his next move. He knew he couldn't find the shooter as an MI6 agent. He would have to go solo.

The limo pulled up to the large stone clubhouse. The driver got out, opened the trunk, and put Cole's golf bag onto the rack outside the front doors. He held the hanger with plastic-covered golf attire in one hand and a shoe bag in the other. He passed them to Buckman after he climbed out of the limo.

"Would you like me to take your sports bag and satchel to your hotel room, sir?"

"Thank you. Pick me up at eight."

"Very good, sir."

Buckman walked into the cool air-conditioned lobby, the size of an airport. A huge cathedral ceiling, large ceramic vases with elaborate bouquets of flowers, cream-coloured couches, and wing-backed chairs made it hard to remember it was a golf club. He quietly disappeared into the men's locker room to change.

Out on the patio, players and caddies and agents and media people milled about drinking sodas or beer. The harder liquor would make an appearance later in the evening. Buckman made his entrance into the sunlight wearing his lucky light mauve golf shirt tucked into his beige slacks, golf glove peeking out of his back pocket, black-and-white golf shoes clicking on the floor. He knew Dustin and Rory were still jealous of the way his body framed his clothes. His short brown hair was hidden underneath his white Nike golf cap. His blue eyes scanned the crowd. He stopped. He wasn't expecting to see her. He had no idea she would be at the tournament.

She was talking to a large group across the patio. He could only see a portion of her profile, but he knew it was her. Her energy danced across the room to meet him. They had played a lot together, golf, among other things. They had spent as much time as possible together, planning their tomorrows. And the next thing he knew, he was driving her to the airport for a mission; she turned out to be an intelligence officer with the military. Amazing how she had kept that a secret from him. She had a small gift for him as he said goodbye, said it was a symbol that they could always be together, just a plane ride away. He thought of the little model airplane tucked inside his satchel. He hadn't seen her in two years. The waiter came up to him. Hard alcohol would start sooner than later for him, just this once.

"Can I get you something, sir?"

"Jack on the rocks," said Cole. It was his drink. "Use the Jack Daniels Sinatra Select, okay?"

"Absolutely."

It was the one drink he couldn't get in Canada, the Sinatra Select version anyway. The waiter walked away, and Buckman turned his head at the exact moment she turned hers. Their eyes met and her face became a morning sunrise. She walked straight toward him, put her hands on either side of his face, and kissed him on the lips, long and hard. Then she stood back and gave him a good slap across the face.

"That's for not finding an airplane in two years."

"Mackenzie Gallo. It's been way too long."

"I won't ask what you're up to, because I know you can't tell me."

"And you wouldn't tell me your latest intel if I had a

gun to your head."

"Well, won't we have a lot to catch up on?" They both laughed and winked. The waiter came and passed Buckman his drink.

"Jack on the rocks?" Mac asked.

"Of course. What else would you drink when you see the woman you loved standing across the room."

"Loved?"

"Okay, okay. Love. It's complicated."

"It's always complicated."

"Wouldn't have it any other way," they said in unison, as if rehearsed. They laughed again, and she leaned her head briefly on his shoulder.

"I've missed you," she said.

"I've missed you too, Mac. What are you doing here?"

"Had a job I had to finish and thought I'd shoot eighteen holes before I left. Found out you'd be playing and thought I'd take a chance."

"On what, seeing me?"

"Well, sometimes you show up, sometimes you don't." She gave him that wry smile only she could muster.

Buckman drank her in. There was still that intensity radiating from her eyes, short light brown hair that she tucked behind delicate ears, that quick wit, a curvaceous body that got his heart pounding. She hadn't changed a bit. "I'm glad you took the chance. Didn't we have a deal?"

"The Vegas deal?"

"The Vegas deal. Exactly. Do you remember?"

She scowled. "I remember important stuff, Buckman. Do you?"

"Every three years, no matter where we are or what we're doing, we meet in Vegas. Details a week before check-in."

"I'm impressed. And I guess that means we could be ahead of schedule."

Buckman glanced around. Some people had noticed him and were starting to look closely. "God, I want to kiss you again, but people are looking. Vegas?"

"You bet your ass. Couple of weeks?"

Buckman nodded.

"Definitely ahead of schedule. Oh, Cole?"

"What?"

"I assume you need a caddy. Near the front of the patio. Anderson. Grab her quick. See you in Vegas, handsome." Mac squeezed his arm, not wanting to let go, and walked over to another group.

Buckman bottomed his glass and walked toward the front of the patio. Mac had been right. There she was. Best investigator any police force could ever have asked for and a computer genius to boot. She was never replaced when she retired early. Irreplaceable. The fact that she had shapely, long legs up to her armpits, breasts that snugged tightly into any blouse, and long, black hair that asked to be wrapped around fingers didn't hold a candle to her talent. Her green eyes missed nothing; they could bore holes into your very being. Plus, she was a fantastic caddy. Being retired from police work, she did that almost full-time. He grabbed her as often as he could on the golf course. They made a great team, and he had won many tournaments with her at his side.

She was engaged in conversation, so Buckman moved in behind her, standing with his back to hers.

"Don't turn around," he whispered.

"Cole Buckman," she said, ignoring and turning.

"How do you do that?" he said. "Eyes in the back of your head?"

"Something like that. Needing a caddy by chance?" She had a low, sultry kind of voice, like warm chocolate sitting in the sun.

"How the fuck did you know?"

"What I do."

"What you did," he reminded her.

"What I do," she corrected him. "By the way, I heard about your dad. How's he doing?"

"I won't ask how you know that… Thanks, yeah, he's out of surgery. In ICU but doing well. He's a tough guy.

Not his first rodeo."

Anderson took his elbow, led him off the patio, and kept walking on the grass. He stayed in step with her. "It wasn't random, Buckman," she said. "The prisoner was the target. Your dad got in the way. But the question is why, or who. And why the fuck was your dad leaving through that door anyway?"

"Funny you mention that... Wait a minute, how the hell do you know all that? Never mind. Don't answer. It's been sticking in my collarbone too. Something smells funny."

"No, something stinks," said Anderson.

"You're not on the force anymore."

"And you can't do a thing as an MI6 agent."

"I was going to ask the agency…"

"Buckman…"

"Yeah, okay, I know, you're right. I have to do this solo. But how the hell am I going to dive into this Pandora's box alone? I mean, was someone actually trying to kill my father? Did he just get lucky? And is he even safe in that hospital? There are a lot of questions."

"And probably a lot more than we've even thought of. You don't have to do this alone."

"What do you mean?"

"Well, there are four of us who love Kitch. You know that. He's always been there for us, and maybe it's payback. They'll come together if you ask nicely."

"But they're all retired."

"Exactly. They're not dead. And they're still the best in their fields. Didn't you see the movie *Red*?"

"Of course."

"I'm just saying. We'd be five. A strong team."

"You're in?"

"Absolutely."

"Could be a C.H.I.L. moment," he smiled, wondering if she remembered. It was something he said right before an intense assignment.

"Courage, honesty, integrity, loyalty. Some things never change." She smiled back. "But first things first, how's your golf swing? Ready to kick some ass?"

MONDAY, MAY 11 | AFTERNOON | BRITAIN

The five key members of the Strike Force had called an emergency in-person meeting. A rare occurrence. They came from various parts of the globe and gathered in one of their safe houses on the outskirts of London, near East Sussex. It was an old thatched cottage sitting alone in the middle of its acreage, with tall oaks and birches completing its privacy. There was a large circular driveway, hidden to other motorists, where black SUVs were now parked. The Strike Force members sat at a large, round wooden table, the only piece of furniture in the room. Men in suits stood on guard at the two entrances to the house, and one remained by each vehicle.

Each member pulled out their small but sharp knife, resembling a tiny sword, and jabbed the tip up into the bottom of the table. It was their code; the small knife, the round table. They had created a design and had it tattooed onto their left shoulder as a show of solidarity and commitment. Commitment to finally putting the world in order. Commitment to ending the tyranny of China. Commitment to justice and honour, like previous knights of the round table in the Middle Ages. They sat back, looking at each other across the table.

"This is *the* election year. What we have been planning for years now. We are so close to changing the leadership around the world."

"Yes, but things have slipped. Why the fuck was Ian at the summit in Toronto anyway?"

"It was dealt with, he…"

"Was shot. Excellent. Is that what we are doing now?"

"If that's what it takes, yes."

"I thought we agreed decisions like that had to be unanimous?"

"I thought we agreed no one would get killed."

"I was never informed. Who ordered this hit?"

Silence in the room as pairs of eyes slid back and forth.

"Someone at this table had to have ordered that execution."

"Maybe not. Maybe it was all a terrible coincidence."

"There are no coincidences. You know that. This was no accident."

"Ian was brilliant. He was our technology expert; he was putting the guts of the plan into motion. What do we do now?"

"Kitch Buckman was his friend. Didn't he recommend Ian to you? Maybe he can step in."

"If he survives."

"That is another question, why was he shot?"

"Well, when mercenaries are involved, concern for human life isn't a high priority."

"Who ordered the hit?"

Dark silence.

"Either no one knows, or one knows, or a few know. I thought we were better than this. I thought we *wanted* to be better than this."

"Things happen. They have to be handled."

"What things? Up to this point, we have been a tight ship, true to the dagger, to the round table. Something isn't right!"

"It doesn't matter. Won't change the fact that he is dead. What matters now is that if we are going to execute our plan, if we are going to actually pull this off, we need a technician as brilliant as Ian, and we need that person right now."

"Do you think Kitch can do it?"

"I don't know. It's not his specialty."

"At this point, we have very few options. Maybe Kitch can replace Ian."

"But Kitch has no idea what's going on. None. Ian never talked with him. We can't bring him on board now. Plus, he's not a computer guy. Barely knows how to work his cell phone. Plus, it's too risky."

"We could bring him in, covertly. Scare him a bit. Give him instructions remotely."

"I think it's our only option at the moment."

"I don't like it."

"What other choice do we have?"

"He gave two names when he was first approached, Ian and a Colin. Colin was nowhere to be found, but we were able to contact Ian, who was very keen on our project."

"Bring him in then. This Colin person."

"Not that easy. There is no data on him anywhere. I've checked, multiple times."

"No photo, no fingerprints, no trace anywhere?"

"None. Just like Ian."

"So we bring Kitch in, covertly, and get him to find him. Threaten him."

Everyone looked at each other.

"We have no choice. We are too close. We need someone to replace Ian. Kitch will have to pay one way or another."

"The price a few pay for the lives of many."

"Precisely."

One of the members was fidgeting, sweating, analyzing his fingernails, clearly uncomfortable.

"Update on the agenda?"

"Hopefully just one more job for that hired Cell and funding will be complete?"

"Let's hope it's just one. Two would be very risky."

"The price of dark web expertise and silence is very, *very* expensive. We knew that."

"The Cell was vetted. One of many. They ask no

questions. They only need to do one more job."

"Then we're done with them."

"We're almost there."

"Almost there? We're talking about taking down a giant, destroying democracy."

"Redirecting democracy."

"It could alter political landscapes forever."

"Precisely."

"Ian had put things into motion. He called it an untraceable whisper campaign via text and social media, shifting the ideas and opinions of the populace. It has begun."

"Any reports?"

"Very, very encouraging. All is on track."

"The hacking initiative is next."

"But we have no Ian."

"Someone better get in touch with Kitch. We need him here. Now. We're all here. He comes to us."

"I'll send word. We'll have him met at the airport."

"This needs to be done quickly."

"While we are all in Europe, let's get him over here."

"We'll meet again in Italy, with Kitch in the room."

"We are taking a huge risk."

"The way I see it, we are taking a huge risk if we don't."

"So, are we done here?"

"We are."

Everyone nodded, but the tension in the room was palpable.

One by one, they pulled their swords out from under the table and in unison stabbed them into the wooden surface.

TUESDAY, MAY 12 | MORNING | CANADA

While Buckman worked with Anderson on the golf course, preparing for competition, Kitch slowly walked the hospital corridors. His body was healing, free of complications. He was lucky. But his mind was busy with complicated, unanswered questions. The biggest of which was what the hell was Ian doing in Toronto, in a courtroom, and not releasing his name? He'd known Ian Duncan a long time. They had met in Ireland years ago. At that time, they had been on opposite teams—Ian with the IRA, Kitch with the government—but they had negotiated together and had developed respect for each other. Even grabbed a pint at the local pub. They were often joined by Colin, the computer expert. Ian said he was opening the world for him. Kitch remembered how Ian was always fiddling with his Glock 27 in his pocket, his little pet, he called it. When Kitch had become lead crown attorney, he had discovered his friend made a shift in career as well, into technology. He had taken Colin's lead. They would meet and catch up when business meetings put them in the same country, which was rare.

Ian had made quite a name for himself in the computer world. When the security advisor to the Canadian prime minister had approached Kitch a few years ago, saying she had a highly sensitive technology situation and needed a kick-ass computer guy, Kitch handed over two names: Ian and Colin. He had been asked for last names and contact info, but Kitch realized he didn't have last names, and only an email for Ian. He gave what he had. He never heard anything and didn't know if either of them even took the job. He didn't know much about Colin, but Kitch knew Ian was proud of what he did and never went the anonymous route, so why the John Doe tactic at the courthouse? It just didn't add up.

If only Cole had not been in court that day, thought Kitch, *I would have got to Ian in time, found out what was going on. He was at the Summit. Why? To speak with the security advisor? But there were no security advisors from any country there.* And then it hit him. That was it. That was why he had been there. Because no security advisors were present. He was there to warn the PM. But why the British PM? There were too many questions with no answers. Cole had been on security detail for the British PM, and he had done his job, as usual. He probably thought Ian intended to kill the PM. He probably had his Glock 27 in his pocket; he took it everywhere. Kitch reasoned it was that weapon that allowed them to arrest him. And whatever he was going to tell the PM was for his ears only. Ian had no love lost for Britain, but he was still a British subject. Had family there. Maybe that was why he wanted to speak with that leader. Kitch couldn't figure it out. Something was missing. Whatever Ian was there to do had got him killed. And then the phone call Kitch received that morning, a request for his presence laced with threat. Info forthcoming. What the hell did it all mean?

He stood still, looking up and down the corridors. Patients moving slowly in wheelchairs, being pushed on gurneys, walking with IV stands on wheels. He remembered the haze of the ICU. A man in a suit standing at the end of his bed, going in and out of focus. *What the fuck is going on?* thought Kitch. He turned back to his room. He got dressed and gathered his things together. He had to think. He had to get home. He also knew he had to be very, very smart right now. "Info forthcoming" flashed onto the screen of his phone.

WEDNESDAY, MAY 13 | AFTERNOON | USA

Cobra and Dangpa shared a room. They had checked into a motel away from the frenzy of downtown Las Vegas. Cobra cleaned her gun, over and over. Since losing part of her left middle finger on a mission while still with the armed forces, she had started cleaning her gun more than once, just to be sure. Now she could only flip people off with her right hand. To protest losing her finger, she got a small serpent tattoo on her left inner wrist. She liked to think it was the devil on her side.

DangPa cleaned her weapon and went over her explosives inventory. She was an explosives expert. The Koreans had trained her well but hadn't treated her that well. Now she used her skill for the highest bidder.

They were each meticulous in their craft. They didn't speak a word to each other. The only sound in the room was the occasional click of metal and the hum of the air-conditioner.

Down the road, Dagger and Berea shared a room in a different motel. They cleaned their weapons and went over the details of the plan, making sure every second was accounted for, every movement smooth and planned. Dagger investigated the security of the Bellagio. His computer skills could hack into anything, anywhere. Berea looked after the smallest of details and vehicles. The drone of the air-conditioner accompanied them, as well as the television news station.

The Cell team had agreed to meet at an out-of-the-way diner down the road for meals and to go over the plan, delegate jobs, and fine-tune the operation. They would do this once a day until the moment of execution arrived. They always met at a different location.

Things were going according to schedule.

THURSDAY, MAY 14 | MORNING | CANADA

Justin Theodore Harrod, or J.T., was out on his John Deere tractor, his green Deere cap shielding the sun from his eyes, doing his morning field check. It was calving time, and sometimes one of the old girls decided to drop a calf behind a rock pile or in the little valley, and if they were having trouble, he wanted to be there to help. He only had a small beef cattle herd. Black Angus. More of a hobby than a livelihood. But he had to do something. He had bought the rambling hundred-acre farm and fixed up the century-old red-brick house, put in a new kitchen, and expanded the living room to accommodate his seventy-inch television screen and leather La-Z-Boy recliners, updated the bathroom upstairs, the plumbing, the electrical circuits, new windows, and a walkout from his bedroom on the second floor. He put up a new farm shed for his tractors and other farm and lawn equipment and a large garage/workshop beside the house. He liked how the light bounced off the pond outside his back door at sunset. He'd sit on his back porch in the evenings in his wooden Muskoka chair, listening to the frogs singing, watching the cows chewing their cud. It was peaceful. It was driving him crazy.

Three hundred kilometres south of J.T.'s farm, Bill Thornton was putting his 45' Outremer Catamaran back into the water. She was a special boat: black hull, black sails, silent electric motors, all so that *Windy Girl* could move from one location to another without attracting attention, especially when moving at night. A black ship blended with the dark waters of Lake Ontario much better than the classic white vessel. It was still rather chilly in the early spring off the coast of Toronto, but he couldn't wait to get back onto his *Windy Girl*. There was always lots to clean and polish, things that needed washing, sails to mount. Lots of work in the days ahead. After that, he'd be sipping a brew with his feet up in the cockpit, a light breeze catching the jib. He loved his sailing and not being in the line of fire every day, but truth be told, he was itching for some action.

One hundred kilometres west of the marina off Toronto Island, Charlie Foster was making a coffee and carrying his newspaper out onto his deck. He never threw a paper out; he might miss something important. He also never threw out a matchbox, a business card, a napkin, or anything else he may have scribbled a note on during an investigation. There were small paths in his living room between the stacks of newspapers and miscellaneous items in boxes, leading to the kitchen, the couch, the front and back door, and the bathroom. It looked like a small labyrinth for Lilliputians. Foster sat down with his coffee and paper on the back deck, listening to the birds singing their spring songs. He wondered what the neighbours would think if he brought out one of his guns and shot the fuckers dead. He could hear the Whipper-Snipper in the yard to his right, the country music in the yard to his left, and a lawnmower in the yard behind him. Privacy was limited in town, regardless of the size of a backyard. He flipped randomly through his paper, sipping his coffee, feeling irritated by all the noise. He was bored.

FRIDAY, MAY 15 | LATE AFTERNOON | USA

Buckman was on the sixteenth hole. He parred the fifteenth, which was a landmark moment for him. Only three holes to go, but he knew he wouldn't make the cut for the weekend. He played better than he expected, so his cover was secure. That was the main goal. And not making the cut wasn't the worst thing. He really felt he had to get back to figuring out what the shooting in Toronto was all about. He had been sent word that his dad checked himself out of the hospital. Sounded about right.

He would finish the course, do the necessary paperwork, drinks, toasts, cheers, goodbyes, and call it an early night. He wanted to catch the early flight home. Anderson had agreed to meet up in Toronto on Sunday. He had a lot of work to do, he thought, walking down the fairway after executing a tremendous drive. Anderson was pulling out his pitching wedge for the next shot. He put his head into the task at hand.

SATURDAY, MAY 16 | MORNING | USA

Buckman sat at Gate 14 at the airport, waiting for his flight. He had easily passed through the security check, having done it hundreds of times, his Sykes knife safe on the side of his leg. His MI6 security team had known how special it was to him and how important to have on a mission. They had made a few improvements; the case Buckman slipped it into made it almost disappear into his calf, aiding its ceramic construction, hence its invisibility through metal detectors or body scanners. His other little treat was his watch. When he couldn't carry a gun, he always had his watch, which could fire very tiny but very poisonous darts.

He leaned back in the uncomfortable hard plastic chair held together with other hard plastic chairs by a thick steel bar, pretending to read his newspaper. Instead, he was reading the room, a habit after years of training. Everything was bolted down in the waiting area, like they thought someone would walk off with an uncomfortable chair or a table or a garbage can. People milled about, pulling luggage, readjusting large bags swung over their shoulders, or checking their fanny packs. Some people were kissing or fighting, crying, sleeping. Some stood at tall tables sipping a coffee or a beer or Scotch; there was no morning or afternoon or evening in an airport, just travel time. Others sat at lower tables where there were adaptors for their technology. There was constant movement. Strands of music occasionally wafted out of small kiosks selling food, books, magazines, souvenirs. The PA system barked out flight delays or calls for missing passengers or to say a flight was boarding. There was a general hum of humanity moving and breathing, fatigue and excitement all rolling around in one large space. Buckman had a way of taking the sound out of a room to listen for the whisper of metal, the click of a weapon, someone holding their breath before making a move. And in that moment, he slowed the whole room down, looked past clothing and eyeglasses, assessing if there was a risk. A virus. Satisfied, he took a breath and allowed the room to come to life again.

He searched for the sports section of the paper in his hand and looked at the golf scores for the tournament. He hadn't won, but he had finished in the top half. He was happy with that. More than acceptable.

He was flying back to Toronto. It was the city where the trail to finding the origins of his dad's bullets began. It was also where he needed to pull his team together. Anderson had been right. He couldn't do this and still be MI6. He needed a team.

He boarded the plane, made his way down the narrow aisle to his window seat, sat down, buckled in, and pulled some papers out of his satchel that he had collected during the week via the computer and printer in his hotel room. His team. They had to be skilled, cunning, dedicated, but more than anything, loyal. Because this wasn't going to be a paid job. This was about looking after one of your own. He started making a list:

Trish Anderson, a.k.a. Falcon. She had already said she was in. She had only retired two years ago and was enjoying life as a caddy for hire. She had joined the police force at age nineteen and quickly became the goddess of technology. Her time spent at Quantico, FBI, in Virginia taught her how to hack any computer or find out who was doing the hacking. She was the best. She was the rock star of the homicide squad, solving case after case due to her skill and tenacity. In her last case, she had worked around the clock for three months to find the guys who killed two civilians in a bank heist. She didn't give up easily. Finally, she had ascertained that there was a link between the bank and the armoured car service through a small coding error. That allowed her to hack into their system, masquerade as one of them, and catch them red-handed. By age forty-four, she had been ready for a change and decided to retire early. *You can take the girl out of the crime world, but you can't the take crime world out of the girl,* thought Cole. She would be a valuable team member.

And Anderson knew Thornton. They had worked together on a few assignments. Bill Thornton, a.k.a. Doc,

55, also retired. Never married. Never had kids. His job was too dangerous. He never allowed himself to get attached. Too risky. For them. For him. Cole remembered his dad often saying he could see Thornton and Trish hooking up. There was something there, Cole had felt it too. But they were professionals. Period.

Thornton had sat in jail cells with the worst of them. Befriended guys who had stuffed bodies in their freezers and then handcuffed them when enough evidence was found. That was what he did. All 6'2" of his 215-pound frame was solid muscle. He had a full head of untamed reddish hair and a beard to match. He wore torn jeans and lumberjack shirts, work boots with the classic Canadian wool socks; grey with the white reinforced toe, white and red stripe around the top. A red toque and down-filled grey vest were added to his wardrobe in the winter. The year before he officially retired, he agreed to train new undercover operatives. His first test was to send the newbies into a bar and have them interact with drug dealers, buy a few bags, get known. One night, waiting for the dealer, his new trainee heard a conversation at the bar, thugs discussing a plot to kill the chief of police. He told Doc what he'd heard the next day. Doc didn't wait. He wasn't the kind of guy that asked permission. And he rarely asked for forgiveness. He showed up at the bar the next night himself and for the next six months became the best friend of the plotters. The day he finally put them in handcuffs was his last day. That summer he had moved into his forty-five-foot sailboat harboured at Toronto Island and rented a cottage on the island during the winter. Buckman hadn't talked to him in ages, but he and Kitch had been very close. He was pretty sure Thornton would be in.

Buckman's team would need a detail man. A forensics magician. The flight attendant interrupted his reverie, asking him if he wanted a drink. He asked for a ginger ale, no ice. She handed it to Buckman, her thumb wrapped around the plastic glass. That was it. Her thumb made him remember. Tuna. Well, his name was Charlie Foster, a.k.a. Tuna. Foster was the evidence genius, highly methodical if not a bit eccentric. A nutty forensic scientist. He could find a tooth filling on a sewer lid. He could also blow up the sewer lid if need be. Foster knew every bomb out there, how to build them, how to defuse them, how to get them. He was meticulous. So, when a fingerprint he had collected as evidence for a big case disappeared, he looked stupid, as did his department, in the middle of court. He vowed that would never happen again. He decided from that point on he would always have the evidence. He would never look the fool again. He began to go to the morgue after the autopsy was complete and before the cremation and cut off the thumb of the victim. That way, he always had proof. He had been known to bring the thumbs in question right into court. Do the print in front of everyone. He became a legend. He went through a few wives. Beautiful women. But they had trouble with the shelves in the basement filled with jars of fingertips and formaldehyde. Fingers mostly from the morgue. but there were most likely criminals walking the street missing a finger or two, suspended in Foster's basement of finger jars. He would be a vital team member.

Finally, Buckman knew he would need a firearms expert. There was only one man for the job: Justin Theodore Harrod, a.k.a. 2Tall. He got his handle from whacking his head, on top of his seven-foot body, on door frames and ceilings. He always looked like a pretzel in any vehicle. He was a dead shot. Knew every gun used in any country in the world and could fire them better than anybody. He'd been a sniper with the special services in the military. Now he trained new recruits. Buckman had worked with him on one assignment. His dad knew him well. He lived on a rambling hundred-acre farm north of Toronto, isolated and well guarded. He didn't like visitors.

Buckman felt the landing gear thud underneath his seat. Rain splattered sideways against the triple-paned window as they approached the terminal in Toronto. He pulled his papers together and stuffed them in his satchel. If they all agreed, he had his team.

SUNDAY, MAY 17 | MORNING | CANADA

They had all agreed to meet at Fran's, an old-fashioned twenty-four-hour diner in downtown Toronto. Breakfast was served all day. Booths with red vinyl benches were separated by beige speckled laminate tabletops with metal trim. A red neon sign flashed *Welcome Home to Fran's* above the door as patrons entered. A glass display case greeted customers, tempting them with slices of cheesecake and apple pie, a few pumpkin, one blueberry. Buckman waited to be seated. The place was already hopping. He took the sound out of the room and scanned it in slow motion: families with kids screaming, older people out for a Sunday breakfast get-together, some solitary people with their phones sitting alone in booths. He zoomed his attention to the solo booths but found nothing of concern. He allowed the sounds to reappear: dishes moving from the kitchen to the tables, hot liquid poured into mugs, cutlery clinking through food onto plates, laughter, breathing, blurs of many words colliding together, sirens on the street, honking cars. A Sunday morning in Toronto.

He appeared to be the first one there. A 40-something woman with brown hair in a curly bob from the fifties, Lucille Ball-style, wearing a grey dress with a red apron tied around her waist, black stockings, and black pumps that showed some nice legs, greeted Buckman and led him to a booth.

"Excuse me," said Cole, "but I am expecting four other people, and one of them would take up that whole bench himself."

"Oh," the waitress said, clicking her gum. She gathered up the menus and led Buckman to a table in the centre of the room with six chairs. She stood looking at him, waiting for his approval, moving the gum to the other side of her mouth.

"Great, thanks," he said.

She started putting the menus down on the table. "Coffee?"

"Thanks." Buckman was visible to anyone coming through the doors. It was busy on a Sunday morning for breakfast, but Buckman liked that. Lots of people, lots of noise, lots of movement, not a lot of opportunity to eavesdrop on a conversation at a nearby table.

The waitress came back and put his coffee in front of him. She dropped a few creamers and packages of sugar beside his cup. Buckman drank his coffee black. He took a few sips, watching the door.

Harrod came in first, ducking his head out of habit as he walked through the doorframe. He wore black Blundstone boots, a dark blue Harry Rosen collared shirt tucked into his slim Levi's jeans, and an expensive leather belt threaded through the belt loops. His hair was still buzzed military-style. He had left his green John Deere cap on the front seat of his truck. As he glanced around the restaurant, he caught Cole's eye and sauntered over. Harrod never wasted energy.

Buckman stood up and extended his hand. "Been a while," he said.

"It has indeed," said Harrod, shaking his hand. They both sat down and the waitress brought another coffee. She smiled at Harrod as she placed it front of him. He smiled back. Buckman looked at the waitress as she walked away, then at Harrod with a lifted eyebrow. Harrod just sipped at his coffee.

"So, how's your dad?" Harrod asked.

"He checked himself out and went home."

"Sounds about right. I'd have done the same."

"Me too. But it was a pretty serious surgery. Just have to wonder if something else forced him to leave so quickly."

"You're thinking…" But before he could finish his sentence, two bear paws had covered his eyes.

"Guess who?" said a deep voice.

"Don't make me flip you onto this table, Thornton. I don't think the waitress would appreciate that."

They laughed as Thornton sat down at the end of the table. He was a grizzly bear in a plaid shirt, jeans, work boots, and the wild red hair and beard of a man long at sea. There was hand-shaking, pats on backs, more coffee, and then Thornton let out a long, slow whistle as his eyes fixed on Trish.

"You're not going to make me blush, Mr. Thornton," Anderson said, walking toward the table, having just entered the restaurant. "You may get a punch though."

Thornton got up and gave Anderson a hug. He noticed how her black slacks hugged her shapely hips and perfect ass, and that her thin cotton sweater swelled in all the right places. She was in great shape. Hadn't changed a bit. He felt that familiar pull toward her and pushed it down, as he had done for years. Her hair was pulled back into a ponytail, and she just wore a hint of copper lipstick and small hoop earrings. She didn't need anything else. She pulled up a chair and sighed as she took a sip of her coffee.

"Foster coming?" asked Thornton.

"So he said," answered Buckman.

"And he's never late," offered Anderson. "By my watch, he has about forty-five seconds left."

They all sat looking at the door while Anderson measured the time. It was as if a gigantic second hand slowly clicked into place, making a deafening thud, and the front door opened. Charlie Foster stepped inside, meticulous to the second, dressed with the same care and detail he gave to his work. Foster walked slowly over to the table wearing his three-piece grey suit, a light blue shirt, and dark purple tie. His greying hair was parted on the left and brushed to the right. He wore black and white socks with a diamond print that were slipped into a pair of black-laced Oxfords. As he sat down, there were high-fives around the table.

"Foster, fucking Foster, nice suit," said Thornton.

"Beautiful suit," said Anderson, stroking his arm and the fabric. Foster smiled.

"How's retirement suiting you, Foster? Getting finger withdrawals yet?" said Harrod.

"Almost daily, big guy. I have a few empty jars jiggling with anticipation. And how about you? I hear you are ruminating with a herd of cows these days. Anything enlightening?" He chuckled.

"Well played, Foster," said Anderson, "well played. What I want to know is how Thornton is still floating around on the big bathtub of his. Haven't fallen overboard yet?"

"God knows it isn't for lack of trying, gorgeous. Where are you hanging your hat these days?"

"That is a secret and undisclosed location at present."

"Still staying in Airbnbs?"

"Yeah."

Everyone laughed. They found it easy to be together, like no time had passed at all.

The waitress came by, standing beside Harrod.

"Any of you want to eat something?" she asked. She'd had her share of coffee-only tables where the stay was long but her tip was small.

"I'll have the bacon and scrambled eggs," said Anderson.

"That's good for me too," said Buckman.

"I'll have the pancakes and bacon," said Thornton.

"That's good for me too," said Foster.

"And you, sir?" She smiled at Harrod.

"The breakfast special, please."

"All of you want toast and home fries with that?" They all nodded in unison. "Great. Thanks. I'll bring more coffee."

As the waitress walked away, as if rehearsed, they all crossed their arms on the edge of the table and leaned in.

"Buckman, you clearly didn't ask us all here just for breakfast," said Thornton.

"No, I didn't."

"The 'Kitch Shooting,' by chance?" asked Thornton.

"Something is off about that shooting outside the courthouse. I'm hearing murmurs," said Foster.

"I'm hearing more than murmurs," said Anderson.

"Murmurs or not, why are we all here?" asked Harrod.

"Okay, let's get right to it," Buckman said. "Something is 'off,' as you said, Foster. Something that almost got my dad killed. I want to find out what. I want to find out why, and I want to find out who."

"And you want us to help you," said Thornton.

"Yes. But more than that, I am proposing that you come out of retirement. I am suggesting we become a team."

"Are you leaving MI6?" asked Harrod.

"I am."

"Will you go back after?" asked Anderson.

"That will depend on a number of variables."

"And you don't know what all those variables are just yet," said Foster.

"Exactly."

"Are you thinking we become a team for more than this one case?"

"That is one of the variables."

They all sat back, sipping their coffees while the waitress put their food in front of them. "Enjoy," she said. The restaurant noise of cutlery on plates and loud voices bounced around the room. They all dug into their food, appreciating the moment to think.

"Damn fine pancakes," said Thornton.

"Agreesh," said Foster.

"That's why you don't talk with your mouth full, Foster," said Anderson. "No one knows what you're saying."

"Well," said Harrod, "my cows don't need me to

babysit them every minute of every day. Kitch has always been there when I needed advice. I want to know what's going on too. I'm in. As far as continuing after, let's see how this goes first. Not sure how I feel about seeing you mugs all the time." He looked back down at his food, poking some home fries onto his fork.

Foster swallowed, looked sideways at Anderson, and continued. "What he said." He nodded toward Harrod.

"I'm in," said Thornton. "Kitch is a good friend. We look after each other."

"I'm in too," said Anderson.

"Do we need a name?" asked Foster.

"No, we don't need a name," answered Harrod.

"Wookies," said Thornton.

Anderson choked on her mouthful of food as she started to laugh. "What?!! You mean like the Chewbacca guy from *Star Wars*? The walking carpet? We don't all look like you, big man."

"Not my problem."

"Fucking brilliant name," said Foster.

Harrod was bobbing his head up and down. "I can live with that. Chewbacca was a fearless warrior. Good to have a team name."

"Wookies; works on a few levels," said Buckman. "Wookies it is. Okay, where do we start, Wookies?" He smiled.

"Don't push it," said Anderson.

"Well, even though that crime scene has probably been scoured, it hasn't been scoured by us. I need to visit that location."

"I'll go with Foster," said Harrod.

"Excellent. And we will need a headquarters of some sort. Anderson will need to set up her mission control centre. Ideas?"

"Well, if we want to stay hidden, with no surprise visitors, I can anchor or moor the boat out of the direct harbour. I already have some pretty upscale technology below deck. Anderson, you are welcome to upgrade."

"That's a great idea, Thornton. Room for all of us below?"

"It's not a life raft, Buckman. She sleeps six."

"Room there is. Okay. Well, Foster and Harrod, you search the crime scene tomorrow. Anderson and Thornton, find the best place to anchor the boat and get mission control set up. I am going to pay my dad a visit. See what he can tell me."

"My guess is not too much," said Harrod.

"Yeah, agreed. And even if he does know something, he won't say, not yet anyway," added Thornton.

"Buckman gets a lot of information just by being in a room," said Anderson. "Not MI6 by accident."

"Our fearless leader," said Foster.

"One other item," said Buckman. "Any of you change

your handles?" They all shook their heads. "Great. When we are on any kind of surveillance or job, only handles used over the airwaves. Agreed?" They all nodded.

They all put their utensils on their empty plates and pushed them to one side, reaching for their refilled coffee mugs. They decided to meet on Thornton's boat on Tuesday, after everyone had a chance to collect some intel.

The waitress came and stood by their table, beginning to collect plates. "Will this be on one bill?"

They all looked at Buckman.

"We don't have an expense account," he said.

"So that's how it's gonna be," said Thornton.

They all got their wallets out and put their share on the table, mumbling, grumbling, and laughing.

Harrod stuffed a twenty-dollar bill into the waitress's apron pocket. She lightly bumped into his arm and smiled.

Breakfast was over, but things had just begun for the Wookies.

CHAPTER TWO

MONDAY, MAY 18 | CANADA

Foster and Harrod wanted to get an early start before the city's vehicle and pedestrian traffic were at full force. They wanted as few eyes as possible. Harrod parked his black Ram 1500 three blocks away and they walked to the courthouse, the rain pounding on the back of their black slickers, their wellies slushing through puddles. Thunder rolled in the distance. It was a full spring storm. They picked up their pace. With rain this hard, things would start to wash away. They wanted to see the street, access point, and laneway on foot. Be able to pause, crouch, gaze, search. Vehicles were too conspicuous. Harrod wanted to see how he would have executed the hit: angles, weapon choice, distance. The rain was definitely a concern. It could wash any evidence clean, hide other items, and fingerprints would disappear. The plus side was that they were well camouflaged, wearing black slickers with hoods up, and when people started coming out, they would all be walking with heads down, umbrellas obscuring their vision.

They arrived at the one-way street that drove past the back door of the courthouse. They didn't need to talk. They both knew their roles. Harrod stayed on the corner. He wanted to look at direction, places for a vehicle to stop, probably a van. He knew it would be ditched by now.

He'd check out the surrounding surveillance cameras later, but he knew there would be no point. The van would be wiped down; the occupants would have changed attire, head to toe. Based on the number of people shot in a very short space of time, he figured it would have been a rapid-fire weapon, submachine gun, and shells would have stayed in the van. But anyone could get a weapon like that. Wouldn't tell him a thing. He needed a projectile. The street had obviously been cleaned up as quickly as possible after the hit. But all he needed was one, and one may have passed right through a body and gone undetected. He started moving to where the prisoner van would have been parked and kept walking past. He calculated how the bullet would change speed and direction after going through a body. He surveyed the street. He slipped on his rubber gloves.

Foster made his way toward the courthouse doors, turtle-style. He had a CN Tower brochure stuffed in his jacket pocket. He'd picked it up from the sightseeing display at Fran's the day before. He pulled it out, clicked his pen, and started to make notes on it, inside his slicker: distance from door to sidewalk, from sidewalk to prisoner vehicle, from prisoner vehicle to crossroad. He stood where he assumed the prisoner would have been standing, then where Kitch would have been standing, and where the guards would have been standing. He wanted all perspectives. He reasoned that Kitch must have been within touching distance of the prisoner, because no one outside a small radius had been hit. Tuna didn't need a measuring tape; he had a built-in scanning system. He stood up, surveying the street. Rain came down harder. He could hear the vehicles spraying through puddles, the deep hum of the streetcars gearing up for rush hour. The dull light of day struggled through the dark, thick rain clouds. He went and stood in the middle of the street, listening. Gurgles and swirls of water rushed to get down the sewer drain. He walked over to the manhole and crouched. He slid on his gloves and began moving the fingers of his right hand over the steel ridges. He felt something move under his fingertip. He put his pointing finger and thumb together, pulling the item into his pinch, and stood up. He dropped it into the palm of his left hand. It was a metal button. There were letters on it, too small to see in the rain. He carefully pulled out a small envelope, dropped the button inside, tucked it into his pocket, then walked in the direction of Harrod.

Harrod slowly moved with the rain past the location where the victims had fallen. He took five or six strides and then pulled out his phone and flipped on the flashlight. He began to weave its beam back and forth in a small area around a doorframe. The light reflected off rain ripples, and then there was a momentary flash. Harrod pulled the beam back slowly until he saw the flash again. There, caught in the wooden edge of the door frame, approximately twenty meters from the scene of the shooting, was a projectile. He smiled to himself. Projectiles that end their journey in a piece of wood keep their shape, and their rifling stays visible. He pulled out his pocketknife and carefully pried the bullet out of the door frame, dropping it into his evidence baggie. He slid the Ziploc closed and tucked it into the pocket of his raincoat.

Foster stood beside the tall man. "Find what you were looking for?"

"I believe so." He grinned.

While Harrod and Foster were at the site, Anderson ventured over on the ferry to meet Thornton at the Toronto Island Marina. There was no other way to get to the island. Thornton waited by the dock in his red F-150. Anderson disembarked from the ferry, pulled her raincoat tightly around her, and ran to his passenger door.

"Guess you're not worried about being spotted in this thing," she said, climbing up into the seat.

"Good morning to you too. I like red, what can I say."

"Man, it's coming down out there."

"Good we're going somewhere that likes water then." He laughed as he pulled out, heading to the harbour. The windshield wipers splashed water off the glass, allowing for a clear spot to see the road ahead. It wasn't far to the parking lot. Thornton pulled into his spot and hopped out, pulling up the collar on his jacket. Anderson came and stood beside him. Some boats were still on dry dock, looking lost and abandoned in their coverings. Ahead was the marina, where boats bobbed in their slip, hugging the walkways between boats, masts swaying back and forth in the wind and rain. Thornton started forward and Anderson followed. They walked along the piers, looking at boats already settled in their berths and empty slips waiting for their buddy. They walked right to the end. *Windy Girl* was written along her side and across the stern. She was beautiful. But Thornton walked right past her and stood at the end of the pier, waiting for Anderson. He pointed out, past the pier into the water.

"There, that's where the moors are fixed. I'll move *Windy Girl* out there. I think it's better than anchoring. More secure and still off the pier. We'll get back and forth with my dingy."

Anderson nodded, shivering slightly.

Thornton turned and headed back to his sailboat. He walked along the side and stepped up onto the boat's deck, turning and offering his hand to Anderson. She took his hand as she stepped up, slipping slightly on the slick surface, having worn the wrong footwear. Thornton steadied her. She looked up and caught his eye, then quickly looked away. He turned into the cockpit.

"Come on," he said. "Let's get out of this wet crap."

She followed him as he opened the hatch to the cabin below, and they both made their way into the belly of the beast.

Anderson took off her hood and shook her hair, looking up. She caught her breath. "Holy fuck. What is this?"

"You don't think I've just been pleasure sailing all this time, do you?"

"Clearly not."

Spread out before her wasn't a cabin with the decorator couch cushions and caviar of a luxury yacht—it was the mission control computer centre of a high-tech operation. Her eyes widened. "This is fucking fantastic, Thornton. Holy shit. This is worth a little orgasm." She walked over and started to lovingly fondle the screens and keyboards.

Thornton approached and handed her a glass. "Here's something to warm you up."

She took the Scotch and happily took a long swig, nodding her thanks.

"Glad you approve," he said. "You're not easily impressed as I recall."

"Bill, this is impressive."

____

Foster and Harrod climbed into the pickup truck. They pulled back their hoods and wiped their faces. Harrod turned on the truck, the heat, and the wipers.

"I called my buddy down at forensics last night," said Foster.

"That pathologist? What was his name?"

"Morty."

"Fuck off."

"Seriously, his name is Mortimer. Worked with him for almost twenty years."

"You can't make this stuff up. Okay, are you thinking…"

"That's exactly what I'm thinking."

"Is he waiting for us?"

"As we speak."

"Still up at Keele and the 401?"

"Yup."

"Grab a coffee first?"

"You read my mind."

While Foster and Harrod drove to the Centre of Forensic Science, Cole stood in the elevator going up to the fifteenth floor of his dad's condo building. He wasn't sure what to expect. He didn't know his dad very well. They stayed in touch over the years, had the occasional lunch or dinner or golf game somewhere in the world where they would meet up, but that was about it. Just small talk. But something wasn't right. Cole could feel it.

The elevator doors opened and Cole walked out, turning down the hall to 1509. He knocked on the door and waited, fiddling with the keys in his pocket. The door opened slowly, cautiously, and there stood his dad. He didn't look well. Drawn. Haggard. Cole just smiled and walked in. Kitch looked down the hall both ways before closing the door and putting up the chain and security latch.

"Wow, gorgeous view of the lake."

"You've never been here before?"

"Never."

It wasn't a huge condo; one bedroom was sectioned off from the rest of the condo with dividers, a small den was tucked inside the front door, and a modern four-piece bathroom stood beside the den. A good-sized living room had a wall of windows overlooking Lake Ontario, with a black leather couch and chair, glass coffee table, and large flat-screen on the wall. A bookshelf to the side of the TV had an array of legal texts with a few Ludlum books tucked here and there. A small stereo sat on the bottom shelf, jazz CDs neatly stacked beside it, and a few Clint Eastwood DVD movies sat on top of the DVD player. There was a galley-sized kitchen behind the living room with white subway tiles, deep grey granite countertops, and stainless-steel appliances. A large balcony faced the lake with a few chairs and a small table neatly tucked at one end. If Cole's mother had still been alive, there would have been plants by the windows, colourful throw pillows on the couch, art on the walls, fresh flowers in a vase on the coffee table, and books everywhere. But she wasn't there.

"Scotch?" asked his dad, walking over to his small bar.

"It isn't even midmorning, Dad."

"For medicinal purposes only."

"You in pain?" asked Cole.

"I'm not feeling like running a marathon this afternoon. Did you want a drink?"

"Any coffee?"

"Hmm, don't think so. Would have to go down the street."

"I'm good with soda, without the Scotch."

Kitch went to work putting ice in two glasses, soda in one, Scotch and soda in another. He came and sat down on the couch, handing the drink to Cole. "You still drink that Sinatra drink? What's it called?"

"Jack on the rocks. Yes, I do."

"That is a good drink. Worth crossing the border for." He took a sip, sucking air through his teeth.

"Why did you leave the hospital, Dad? You don't look

so good."

"Didn't like it in there. Didn't need to be there." He looked into his glass for answers, for time. He didn't know what was coming, and he didn't want Cole involved. He'd received a very cryptic message telling him about a flight he needed to be on the next day, departing to Italy. He would be given more instructions upon arrival. He was told to speak to no one. He was told to be on that flight. He was told the other option was to become roommates with Ian.

"Did anyone other than me come to visit you there?"

Kitch looked up. "Why all these questions?"

"Something doesn't feel right, Dad. I'm concerned the stray bullets that hit you might not miss next time."

Kitch looked back into his golden liquid. He swirled it around the melting ice cube, watching it change shape. He took another sip and spoke while looking into the glass. "They were stray bullets, Cole." He looked directly into Cole's eyes. "Leave it at that." He got up off the couch and walked to the kitchen island, emptying his glass, and putting it down. "I'm a bit tired. I think I'm going to lie down for a bit." He started toward the front door, opening it.

Cole got up off the couch. He walked over and stood in front of his father, then leaned forward and hugged him. His dad hugged him back. Cole could feel him flinch in pain. He said nothing, stepped back, and smiled. "Look after yourself, Dad. I'm off on assignment tomorrow. Be C.H.I.L."

Kitch laughed for the first time that morning. "Remember when we invented that acronym?"

"How could I forget? It was the year our team made the hockey championships. I was feeling a lot of pressure and not keeping my cool."

"You were only twelve."

"Twelve. Yeah. And you came over to the bench, which you weren't supposed to do, and waved me over. All you said was be C.H.I.L. I had no idea what you meant. But you smiled, patted me on the shoulder, and said you'd explain after the game."

"You won that game. Scored the winning goal, as I recall."

"I did. And I've used C.H.I.L. ever since: in sports, during exams, and even with teams on clandestine missions. It's my 'thing' now, apparently."

"Always a good thing: courage, honesty, integrity, loyalty."

"Always a good thing," said Cole.

The mood shifted and became cloaked again.

Cole stepped out into the hall and looked back. "Love you, Dad."

"Love you too, son."

"See ya."

The door closed, and Cole walked toward the elevator. There was some serious shit going down. He imagined finding the guy who did all this, bouncing his head off a door frame, and then planting his elbow firmly into the guy's left eye. His eyeball would be hanging by a thread from the socket. The guy would stagger, reaching for invisible supports. Cole wouldn't hesitate. He'd wheel around, planting his foot below his other eye and into the side of his nose that connected with the front of his jaw. Blood would fall out behind the teeth onto the beige hall carpet. Hands fisted together, he'd thump him at the base of his skull and leave him balled on the floor.

The elevator doors opened, and Cole stepped inside, his muscles tense, his jaw clenched.

He knew what had to be done.

Harrod pulled onto Keele Street. The Tim Hortons donut bag and wrappers were compressed into a ball and had been tossed onto the floor in the back seat. Harrod and Foster both liked the apple fritters. They finished off their Timmie's coffee as they pulled into the lower level of the Centre of Forensic Science building. The empty cups found their way beside the donut wrappers.

The Centre was like a second home to Foster. He and

Mortimer Foley had met when they were both at the beginning of their careers. They often helped each other out over the years. Mortimer always said he would never retire. He liked his job too much. Besides, he always said, after cutting up dead bodies for so long, he really wasn't that good with the live ones. Especially if they were female. A lonely profession.

They pulled into a parking spot, hopped out of the truck, beeped it locked with the key fob, and made their way to the ramp. Everything was designed to make the movement of heavy, dead bodies easier. No stairs. Right from the parking lot, to a ramp, to the mortuary. Morty met them at the entrance wearing a white lab coat stained with the faded blood from jobs that morning and probably the day before. Blue and red plaid slacks stretched out below the lab coat. He wore round wire-rimmed glasses and had his thinning grey hair pulled back into a ponytail. He had a platform on the sole of his left white Converse running shoe to account for his LLD—leg length discrepancy. He'd had it since he was a child. His parents had rejected trimming the bone back on his longer leg, and instead had a custom shoe made for his left foot. He had endured teasing throughout his life, turning him to solitary work as an adult. He was pale and appeared to be gazing straight ahead at nothing.

Foster never gave a damn about the platform shoe.

"Morty, how have you been?" he asked, reaching forward to shake his hand.

Morty looked down at Foster's hand, back up at his face, almost smiled, and brought his hand up to meet Foster's. "Could be better, could be worse."

"Isn't that what you always say?"

"No point in changing a good thing." Morty looked up at Harrod.

"Morty, meet my good friend and colleague, Harrod, J.T. Harrod. J.T., Morty." After a brief hesitation on both parts, they extended their hands and shook.

"Nice to meet you, Morty," he said. "Thanks for your help on this one."

Morty turned and walked inside the building. Harrod followed Foster, looking around him at Morty.

"I understand you are interested in the unidentified body taking space up in my office," he said, walking down the hall, his back to Foster and Harrod.

"Can we have a look?" asked Foster.

"Police were here," he said, turning into the lab.

Foster and Harrod followed him in. The door closed behind them. The room was white and grey. Cupboards with glass doors stood on one wall, large refrigerator doors one on top of the other, on another wall. One lone metal desk with drawers on either side, a laptop, printer, other complicated-looking equipment, some paper, pens, a water bottle, and what looked like a lunch bag sat on the top. Three stainless steel trays that stood waist-high were in various places in the room. Uncomfortable-looking surgical devices sat perfectly organized on the trays. The lighting was blinding and reflected off all the metal. There was a soupy smell of decay and coffee and embalming solvents that floated into their nostrils. Harrod swallowed hard, trying to keep his apple fritter down.

"I took the fingerprints and other details off the body," Morty said. "Sent them over. Haven't heard anything since then. Fun fact: he had a coating, invisible to the naked eye, on his fingertips. A lot of criminals wear it now, easier than putting on gloves all the time, I guess. So, if they tried to get an ID on him when he was arrested, fingerprints would not have helped. Nothing would have come up. I had to peel off that coating and take new fingerprints. All in all, it was a pretty messy job. Kinda fun. It can get a little dull in here."

Morty went over to a tray and picked up a pair of surgical gloves, pulling them onto his fingers very precisely and finally snapping the band onto his wrist. He walked over to a wall outfitted with large, square, refrigerator-style doors, about ten in total. He reached for one in the centre, opened it, and pulled out a stretcher with a covered body on it. He pulled the cover back and proudly began talking about his work. "This was a fucking mess, lads, before I did my magic. There was a lot of disconnected skin, shall we say, on his torso. Bullets must have been dancing all over the place and fired at very close range. There was a lot of tattooing."

"Tattooing?" asked Harrod.

"Tattooing," repeated Morty. "When bullets embed burnt particles in the skin. And there were a lot of flame burns. The guards they brought in looked pretty similar, but not as bad as this guy. Let's just say it's a good thing they still had fingers and teeth, because you wouldn't have identified them easily by facial recognition. So, it wasn't a big stretch, excuse the pun, to open him up and deal with his organs. Except that not many of his organs were intact either. Fucking mess. I did find a projectile lodged in his shoulder, but police have that now."

"Did that projectile look anything like this?" Harrod pulled the small plastic bag from his pocket holding the treasure from that morning's hunt. He put it in the palm of his hand, extending it toward Morty. Morty needed to confirm it was the same bullet that he took out of the guy's shoulder, otherwise it could really be any bullet from any point in time and maybe worth nothing except a wild goose chase.

Morty leaned over and peered closely into Harrod's hand. He stepped back and looked up at Harrod. "Yup, that's it. Same surplus steel-core 9mm. Yeah, that's the same one. Not common. I couldn't place the weapon."

Harrod affectionately closed his fingers around the little projectile safely zipped in the baggie and carefully put it back into his pocket. He had his own ideas about the weapon it had come from.

Morty turned back to the body. "I had to saw through the skull and make an assessment of the damage. The brain was spaghettied. Not much else to see. I peeled the skin back from the face to see if there was any other cranial damage. But I already knew what I would find… more mess."

Harrod tried not to hold his breath, looking at the stitches around the side of the victim's face. Morgues were definitely not his comfort zone.

"I then reattached the skull and stitched him back together," said Morty.

Foster stood beside Morty. "Nice work here, Morty. This would not have been an easy makeover."

Morty almost smiled again. "Harrod, want to have a closer look?"

Harrod put his hand up and waved Foster off, looking the other way. He didn't trust himself to speak at that moment. Harrod was a gun expert. This wasn't a gun, and he was looking a little bit green.

Foster stifled a chuckle as he leaned back over the body, doing some poking and prodding of his own, complimenting Morty on some very fine stitching.

Just seeing the body lying on the table like that took Harrod into a haunting memory. He could feel the vibration and roar of the Black Hawk helicopter as he sat in the back with the rest of the special forces team. They were being sent to rescue US and Canadian civilians in the Middle East. The LZ, landing zone, was being cleared by twelve US Rangers so the choppers could land safely. But before the choppers could touch down, all twelve rangers were killed by enemy soldiers. The special forces team exited the chopper before it landed, taking out the rebel soldiers swiftly and securing most of the civilians, but even more team members were lost. At the end of the day, the bodies were lined up side by side at the edge of the LZ, and it was a gruesome sight: arms missing, pieces gone off faces, legs blown off, blood everywhere. There was nothing to cover them with until the next choppers came that would carry them home, but Harrod was long gone before that happened. To him, it was a morgue from hell, so morgues weren't his favourite places. Most special forces veterans kept their nightmares to themselves, and they had many.

"Police aren't releasing any information at present," said Morty. "I'd really like to free up some space in here. Don't know why this is taking so long."

Foster looked over at Harrod. It was a point worth

remembering. "Would love to help you out with that, Morty my man, but sadly, you'll have to wait on the police for that. This is an under-the-table situation. I'm retired."

Foster looked at Morty. Morty looked at Foster. They winked at the same time. Harrod just looked. Morty turned and went to a tray where stainless steel tools were carefully laid out. He picked up a pair of what looked like small pruning shears and handed them to Foster. Harrod looked at the tray. He'd seen those used on people that hadn't made it to the morgue yet. Somehow, that was easier to stomach than what happened in that lab room.

"Would you like to do the honours?" Morty asked Foster.

"I'd be honoured," Foster replied. He took the scissors, picked up the corpse's hand, one of the few body parts that hadn't been shredded, and snipped off the left thumb like he was pruning a garden shrub. Morty handed him a small Ziploc baggie containing a small amount of formaldehyde. Foster put the finger in the bag, zipped it closed, and tucked it into his pocket, not the one with the button.

"Will that go in the jar collection?" asked Morty.

"Of course, after we figure out who this guy is."

"Would you like me to do a quick scan? I can't access the records already filed in the database, but I can print you a new one. All on the QT, of course."

"Of course."

"Hang on to that thumb, Foster, you know, just in case. Computers are fallible."

"That's why I have the jars." He grinned.

Harrod was looking more than a little green.

"I'll get a print from his other hand before we slide him back." Morty went to work getting the fingerprint and then scanned it into the system. Within seconds, there was the whirring sound of the printer jumping into action, and two pieces of paper slid forward. Morty picked them up, folded them in half without looking at them, and passed them to Foster, who tucked them into the inside pocket of his suit jacket.

Morty covered up the corpse and pushed the tray back into the wall, closed the fridge door, walked back over to his desk, peeled off the gloves, and dropped them in the garbage can before taking a drink from his water bottle.

He walked out of the lab and started down the hall, Foster and Harrod following behind. Not a word was spoken. The only sound was the echoes of their feet down a long, pale yellow concrete corridor.

"It's pretty quiet in here on a Monday morning," said Morty as he walked ahead of the other two, "but I wouldn't linger too long."

"We're on our way," said Foster. They all stopped at the door to the garage. "Thanks, Morty. Next time."

Morty just stood, staring ahead at seemingly nothing again. "See ya," he said and turned to walk back to the lab. He had a Rice Krispie square in his lunch bag that was calling to him.

Harrod climbed into the driver's seat while Foster settled into the passenger seat.

They pulled out of the garage and made a left onto Keele. Foster pulled out the brochure he had used to jot down his notes earlier outside the courthouse and he scribbled some ideas on another corner of the paper. Once on the road, Harrod exhaled deeply.

"Is that the first breath you've taken since we went in?" asked Foster.

"I think so."

TUESDAY, MAY 19 | CANADA

The *Windy Girl* was moored outside the marina. Thornton had maneuvered a satellite reception device on the top of the mast, making all computer connections fast and seamless. Anderson demanded it. She said she couldn't work if the system had a pause or a hesitation. That was when uninvited guests appeared through the technological cracks. They knew time was ticking and so made things happen fast. Everything was up to her standards by Tuesday afternoon.

It was a calm day on the lake. The storm the day before had passed through, leaving warmer spring breezes behind but cloudy skies. It was a dullish kind of day. The Wookies all found different ways of getting to Thornton's boat that afternoon. Harrod had considered swimming but decided the lake was still too cold. He paddled over with Foster. By 2:00 p.m. they were all sitting below deck, sipping on their drink of choice.

Foster unbuttoned his jacket and reached into the inside left pocket, pulling out a pen and the brochure. He flattened it out on the table and pushed his coffee to one side.

"Graduated past match book covers?" teased Thornton.

Foster ignored him. "The victims were all standing pretty close together, based on my calculations. And they were in pretty close range to the shooter."

"That also became clear when we saw the body," said Harrod.

"Apparently we need to make sure we send some air sick bags with you next time you have to visit the morgue," said Anderson.

"Very funny. But yes, air sick bags would be a good idea." They all laughed. "Not my favourite place, but definitely good Foster has this buddy Morty." He put the bullet on the tabletop. "Morty was able to confirm this was the same bullet that came out of the corpse's shoulder."

"So we know it's from the same gun. Could Morty tell you what gun?" asked Thornton.

"No. But those wounds, and the ones sustained by the guards, that was from a submachine gun. At least four hundred rounds per minute. That's about seven rounds a second."

"That's a lot of bullets in a short time," said Anderson.

"Exactly," said Foster. "And at close range, as I suspect they were, the damage would be magnified, as we saw."

"We need to know what gun was used," said Buckman.

"My thoughts exactly," said Harrod. "I did some digging and noticed the rifling on this projectile is counterclockwise, not common. And when I took into account the wounds on the body, well, it can only be one weapon, and it's rare."

"Rare is good," said Thornton. "I like rare. Easier to sniff out."

"What is it?" asked Buckman.

"It has to be the very rare FNAB-43, a submachine gun made between 1943 and 1945. There weren't many made because they used extensive milling and precision engineering, so it was really expensive to manufacture. It was used by a very elite group of German and Italian soldiers in Northern Italy during the war. They pop up now and again. The weapon, not the soldiers. They are a bit of a legend. Again, the weapon, but maybe the soldiers too. Many have heard about them but never held one in their hands. Yours truly included. They are like a rare painting, but in the gun world. Now, their cost is astronomical, but their performance is still extraordinary. I want to know who this shooter is and how the hell they got their hands on this weapon."

"And why are they firing it in Toronto?"

"Kitch would have been standing within arm's reach of this guy when the shooting started. It's lucky he wasn't close enough to smell his breath. He would have been on a different stretcher," said Foster.

"How many bullets did he sustain, Buckman?" Anderson asked.

"I'm not exactly sure, but he got a good spray."

Thornton passed Buckman another beer and got one for himself. Foster got up to refill his coffee mug and Harrod's. Anderson sipped her Perrier.

"How is he?" asked Anderson.

"Cautious," said Buckman.

"Then you're not going to want to hear this," she said.

"Hear what?" asked Buckman.

"He's boarding a flight to Italy this afternoon."

"What?" Buckman, Thornton, Harrod, and Foster all said together.

"I've put a cyber tail on Kitch," said Anderson. "If we're going to find out what he's got himself involved with, we better know where he is."

"Wow, didn't take you long to get this gear up and running."

"Part of my job, boys."

"May I say," said Foster, "this is a fucking amazing outfit in here. Talk about mission control. I feel like I'm in the *Millennium Falcon*."

Thornton slapped him on the back, laughing. "Fuck. I love it. Maybe I should change the name of the boat."

"It's very high-tech, I'm impressed," said Buckman. "Okay. So, he's off to Italy. Why the hell is he off to Italy?"

"I also found a strange private jet that left for Vegas a

few day ago."

"Why are you bringing that up?" asked Thornton.

"Right now, I'm fishing for anything suspicious and odd. This is odd because it appears to be a last-minute entry."

"That happens a lot with these rich folks," said Harrod.

"Yeah, but they weren't rich folks; they were musicians and they aren't booked to play in Vegas."

"Maybe they're taking a vacay," said Foster.

"Maybe they're not. I'll get a flight to Vegas," said Buckman.

"You don't even know who you're looking for," said Harrod.

"I rarely do," said Buckman.

The boat swayed in its mooring. They all steadied their drinks. "Do you need a sick bag, Harrod?" asked Anderson.

"I'm good. I'm good," he said. "Boats are fine, unless you have a cut-up corpse in the back there."

"That can be arranged," said Foster. He smiled and sipped his coffee.

"We have another little piece for the puzzle. You're gonna like this." Harrod looked over at Foster, who reached into his pocket and pulled out the button, placing it dramatically onto the table. They all leaned forward, peering at the object.

"What is it?" asked Anderson.

"It's a button Foster found."

"A button?" said Thornton.

"Harrod makes it far more than a button." He turned to Harrod.

"Foster showed me the button when we went for a coffee after the morgue. I recognized it immediately. It's from a special forces shirt. Everyone was issued one. The writing on the button indicates what unit they were with. No one wore them in combat. It was something that distinguished us, sort of like a badge of honour."

"So, what you're saying is the button might have come off the shirt of the shooter," said Anderson.

"Or someone else in the van," said Buckman.

"Exactly," said Harrod.

"Can you find out who was in that particular unit?" asked Thornton.

"The wheels are already in motion," he said.

"Well, my Wookies, that's some pretty great work for one day. We all done?"

"Not quite," said Foster. He looked back down at his scrawled notes on the brochure. "Morty said he didn't know why the police were taking so long to release the corpse's identity. Odd. For some reason, they don't want him cremated just yet. Why?"

"Why indeed," said Buckman. "I've seen my father be crafty and cunning, but never this. This is a dark kind of cautious. I've seen it before. Something is up. Who was that guy they were shooting at? Why did they want him dead?"

"And why was Kitch trying to talk to him?"

"Who is he?" asked Anderson.

"Well, we will always be able to find out, because Foster has his thumb in a jar in his basement collection."

"*What?*" they all said in unison again.

"Of course I have his thumb. Interesting situation. Morty mentioned that the vic had a coating on his fingertips, impossible to see or feel but also made it impossible to get an ID from a fingerprint."

"Yeah, I heard about that on an undercover op I did," said Thornton. "That's how the perps are walking free so often. How did he get the prints?"

"Morty looks for that now, and then he peels it off with one of his tools."

Harrod just closed his eyes.

"And this little thumb is coating-free, you know, in case things go missing. Just good planning. It's what I do." Foster put the bag on the table, and the Wookies gathered to have a look to see if they could tell where the coating had been peeled off.

Foster may have been a bit unorthodox in his

methods, but he was one of Canada's most well-respected CSI police officers, and he remembered exactly when he had decided on that goal. It all began with Cynthia, a girl he fell in love with in high school, and a dry cleaner where she worked part-time. The local officers had their uniforms cleaned at that place, and a local gang was looking to pick up some of those uniforms. A thug in a police uniform could get what he wanted more easily, for a while at least. Cynthia usually worked there after school, did her homework, and closed up at eight. But that one night she decided to stay a bit later and finish her homework assignment before heading out. She locked up at eight and kept working in the back. At 8:55 she gathered her stuff together and left through the back door, backpack slung over her shoulder, walking right into the gang members. They pistol-whipped her, striking her in the head several times, and left her bleeding in the alley while they went to get the uniforms and any cash they could find. Charlie had been calling her since eight, and her parents were a bit worried, so he decided to head over to the dry cleaner. He peered in through the window and saw things in disarray, so he went around to the back door, and there she was, bleeding out in the street. Charlie was told later that he saved her life by getting her to the hospital so fast, but because of the blows to the head, she lost her sight permanently. The police investigation had been botched from the get-go. No charges were ever laid. Fingerprints were lost. It was a shit-show. At that moment, Charlie decided he would become the best CSI officer, and criminals would have to think twice.

"Can't even see where he peeled off the coating," said Anderson, bringing Foster out of his reverie. "Although it is kinda creepy, I see why you keep the fingers," she added reluctantly.

"It's my insurance if technology goes tits-up, or I lose this…" Foster pulled out the folded paper that Morty had handed him before they left the morgue. He opened it up. "Morty printed this off for me. Took the corpse's fingerprint and put it through the system while we waited. His name is right here. Anyone know an Ian Duncan?"

WEDNESDAY, MAY 20 | ITALY

Kitch Buckman cleared customs in Leonardo da Vinci International Airport. He was quickly met by a tall man in a suit. A fuzzy image crept into Kitch's mind, a dim memory, as he followed the man out of the airport. He struggled to reach the memory, like wanting to grasp something in a dream that keeps fading in and out. As the man turned to open the back door of the sedan for Kitch, a wasp of a memory stung him: a tall man in a suit, reaching for the rails at the end of his hospital bed in the ICU, leaning forward, watching Kitch as his sedation only allowed him to drift in and out of consciousness. It was the same man opening the door of the sedan. Kitch felt a winter chill sweep over his body, like he had just stepped against a thin crack on lake ice and was plunged into the freezing waters below. He was in over his head.

THURSDAY, MAY 21 | USA

Cobra disassembled her weapon carefully and placed each section into its spot in the case. The individual compartments were concealed under the instrument itself, and the hard case was then locked. Each member had done the same with their weapons, and a few other pieces that would amass chaos and destruction if needed: smoke grenades, tear gas, flashbang grenades. These would wait for them in the motel room for later. The disposable guns they needed for the job Saturday night were stowed in bins, already waiting in the car.

They had been directed to only use force and chaos as needed. Their objective: cage money. The big UFC fight on Saturday was their invitation.

They met in the diner for lunch.

"Are the masks ready?"

"I'm picking them up later today."

"Are we all paying with cash?"

"And we're all giving the same phoney name? No handles, no real names."

"Nope. We're all Frankie Best."

"Good. Banners?"

"Boxed and waiting under the bed."

"Status?"

"Everything is booked for the fight. Doesn't look like

a spare room anywhere in Vegas."

"Bets have already begun to pour in."

"Money will accumulate quickly. It's a big weekend for Vegas."

"Berea, brown clothes and caps in place?"

"Affirmative."

"Dagger, do you have control over the security systems?"

"I do."

"How long will we have?"

"Nine minutes. One minute in the cage. One minute to get out. Seven to get to the waiting vehicle outside."

"Amy, explosives ready if needed?"

"Always."

"Berea, getaway driver arranged?"

"He was a little greedier than I wanted, but yes."

"Well, that's an easy problem to solve."

"He won't be having dinner later that night."

"Get a good sleep tonight. Rest up tomorrow. No one leaves their hotel room. Get whatever you need today."

"We'll meet outside the Bellagio, 8:00 p.m. Saturday."

While the Cell went over details of their next job, Kitch was being led out of the sedan, his hands handcuffed behind his back, a thick black hood over his head. He felt like he was underwater in winter, trying to find a crack in the ice for air. *Focus,* he kept telling himself, *focus*. While driving, he counted the number of stops that were made, long stretches of driving, turns. But he had no way of knowing what direction he was travelling. He was getting nauseous with the bag over his head and it was hard to breathe. When he got out of the car he heard the odd dog bark and an occasional cow lowing, which told him they were definitely out of the city, but other than that, he had nothing.

He tripped as the hand on his back directed him into a large room. He could tell it was large by the way his footsteps suddenly echoed. A warehouse, maybe a renovated barn. What he couldn't see were the five people sitting at a round table in the centre of the otherwise bare room, windows all covered. A man in a suit stood at the door on the far side of the room, guarding the only other door. The man that picked Kitch up at the airport led him over to a chair. He then moved to stand by the door where they had entered. In all his years of cases as a Crown attorney, in all his encounters with the IRA, in all his years in service, never had he felt cold sweat running down his spine like he felt as he sat in that chair, God knew where. He could only wonder what Ian had gotten himself into. He thought back to "Kitch's Law." Right now, he felt a need to rework that law: shoot first, ask questions later. If only he had a weapon.

"Mr. Buckman. We apologize for the hood and handcuffs. We felt it would be better this way," said a man with a French accent.

"Less you know, the better," said a woman.

Canadian or American, hard to tell, thought Kitch. *Definitely not European or Asian.*

"You mean so I don't end up like Ian. I assume that is why I am here."

"You are correct."

Same woman, thought Kitch. He was trying to ascertain how many people were in the room and who they were.

Voices came from different places at what Kitch guessed was a table. His head turned automatically when he heard a sound, as he stared into the black of the hood, light peeking through the thick weave of the fabric. He pulled on his hands inside the handcuffs.

"So why am I here?" he asked.

"We understand you are a close friend of Ian."

Another's woman's voice. British accent. "I *was* a close a friend," he said.

"Yes, was. Regrettable. Did he ever speak about his work with you?" *Another man's voice.*

"Never. Much of what we did was confidential. We rarely talked about work."

"You referred him."

"What does that have to do with anything? That was a confidential meeting I had, a couple of years ago. I didn't even know what the job was. I just gave two names; Ian's and a friend of his, Colin. I was told a computer expert was needed."

"Yes. Simply put, Mr. Buckman, you need to carry on for your friend."

"I *what*?" said Kitch, his eyes popped open inside the hood. Beads of sweat ran into his eyes. He had no way to wipe them away. "You can't be serious. Carry on what?"

"We are dead serious." It was like a simultaneous breath was taken.

"You referred Ian because of his work with the IRA and his computer skills. Correct?" *A raspy male voice, thick Italian accent.*

"Nothing was said about the IRA. How did you know that?"

"Well, we know you worked with Ian with regard to IRA disputes in the past. We assume Ian shared his computer savvy with you."

"You assume incorrectly. What did Ian actually do for you?"

A long, pondering silence. A woman answered, not the British one. "He was our digital director, you could say."

"And now you will need to take on that role." *A new voice. Male. American.*

"And how do you propose I do that? I am a lawyer. I know very little about computers," said Kitch.

"This is not a request."

"I have extremely limited technological knowledge," Kitch whispered to himself. Nausea formed in his gut.

"We know you have resources. You'll find someone. You suggested Ian. You also suggested Colin. Find him."

"He is a ghost. Even if I could find him, what do I tell him exactly?" asked Kitch. Anger and outrage began to replace his fear. He had heard at least five voices, but it was hard to be certain. At least two women, men with accents. Some were smoking. He couldn't tell what. One voice sounded almost familiar, but there was too much going on in his brain to process and distinguish between the voices. He wished Cole were there. He would be able to isolate and identify each voice. No situation got him flustered.

"You will think of something. You're a clever man."

"But still, what am I asking? What was Ian doing?" asked Kitch.

"Digital director."

"Directing what, exactly?"

"We will give you specific instructions when and as needed."

"Tell your contact you need someone well versed in the dark web and with the know-how to hack into any system and database. Ian has already launched his, shall we say, architecture. You will be brought up to speed on that and given suggestions on how to continue and implement his detailed plan."

"Oh, is that all? How do I contact you if I find someone?" asked Kitch.

"Maybe the hood is affecting your hearing Mr. Buckman. It is not an 'if'—it is a 'when.' And a 'when' within the next seven days. And you don't contact us, we will contact you."

"You want me to find Colin to replace Ian in one week. What will the payment be? It will be a question," said Kitch.

"It will be worth his while. After our first meeting together, we will present the renumeration package."

"Renumeration package. Sounds like a life-or-death annuity," said Kitch.

No answer.

"We will be in touch. Make sure you have his name for us."

"You have to give me some time."

"One week. We need a name in one week. Time is pressing."

"I thought you were kidding. A week. Seriously?"

"One week."

"We will contact you in a week."

"And if I don't have anything, will I be bunkmates with Ian?"

"You'll have something." It was that female voice again. Kitch rolled his eyes around trying to place it.

The next thing Kitch knew, a hand gripped his arm, pulling him to standing. The hand on his back directed him out of the room. He found himself back in the sedan. The car began to move.

He felt like the ice had closed over his head.

FRIDAY, MAY 22 | CANADA

Cole Buckman secured his seatbelt as the aircraft taxied to the runway at Pearson International Airport. He had a lot to mull over. He wanted to know why his father was on a plane to Italy after checking out of the hospital earlier than recommended. He wanted to know who it was that Anderson picked up on her computer chatter, travelling on a private plane to Vegas. Something must have really been out of the ordinary for Anderson even to mention that flight. Why were the police not releasing the name of Ian Duncan? Buckman thought back to the meeting on *Windy Girl*. Fantastic boat. Fantastic setup. Fantastic team. In such a short time, they had already uncovered so much. Now it was his turn. He was flying into Vegas blind for the most part. It wasn't the first time he had found himself on such a mission, with little to no intel. He put his back against the headrest and closed his eyes.

He had only been on a few missions as an MI6 agent back then. The British prime minister had sent his most trusted advisor as an envoy to negotiate the release of a high-profile British subject held prisoner by a faction in the Middle East. Within hours, the advisor had been taken prisoner as well. Buckman was assigned to the extraction mission, along with the United Kingdom's special forces team, the SAS. Cole's stealth abilities were gaining recognition. It was the reason he had been assigned. They needed someone highly trained in combat, with a unique innate ability at surveillance: Cole Buckman. Reports said twenty to thirty hostage-takers were guarding the prisoners held in a storage structure about the size of a small barn. Smaller adjacent buildings would be where the hostage-takers were sleeping. Buckman and the rest of the team were dropped by helicopter at 12:30 hours, eight kilometres from where the prisoners were being held. The night was darker than black coffee. They wore black camo fatigues, rubber-soled combat boots, tactical gloves, and load-bearing body armour filled with mags and med supplies. AR-15s were slung over their shoulders. Buckman adjusted his night vision goggles, tightened his helmet, and slung his C8 over his shoulder. His trusty stiletto knife was strapped to his lower leg. No other countries had been informed of this British covert mission. The PM wanted his envoy and the British prisoner out. Period. Buckman remembered how hard it was to move quickly and quietly wearing all that gear. He was used to working alone, in street clothes. His radar was on high alert.

He and his SAS partner would take out the night guards, Buckman front, the other back. It was dark, quiet, and no one in the area was expecting visitors. Buckman moved silently, came up behind the guard, grabbed his head, and in one swift motion broke his neck. Soundless. He motioned to his partner. It was agreed that Buckman and his partner would go in and extract the two prisoners while other members of the team set explosives on the doors and windows of the other buildings. They would be set off if a quiet escape was compromised.

Buckman recalled the stunned look on the envoy's face as he entered the room. The envoy sat on a dirt floor in a room that smelled like a latrine. There was blood on his face and his clothes were torn. Buckman placed his fingers across his lips, took the man by the arm, and started to lead him out. He stopped when he heard the voice of his partner in the adjoining room trying to quiet the other British prisoner. He was spooked, in shock, refusing to leave. Terrified of reprisal. Buckman cringed. He would have knocked him out and slung him over his shoulder. Instantly. Noise was the enemy. But his partner had hesitated. And sure as shit, the prisoner's yelling started to wake the hostage-takers one by one. Shots were fired, and the prisoner went down. Buckman's partner took a bullet in the leg. Buckman ran over, dragging the envoy with one hand, and pulled up his partner with the other. He yelled out the code word, and doors and windows started to blow off buildings. Buckman radioed the chopper and said they would be coming in hot; they were taking fire.

The hostage-takers were close behind and firing. Two other SAS members went down, when out of nowhere Buckman saw two more coming directly toward him. He dropped his partner and the envoy, whipped his rifle into his hands, and started firing. The rest of the team kept firing while one went over to help drag Buckman's wounded partner and the envoy to where the chopper would land. Lights flooded the ground, as did bullets from the chopper. It hovered as low as possible while Buckman pushed the envoy onboard and then went back for his partner. He grabbed him by the collar and started dragging him back. Explosives fired and guns blared when Buckman grabbed the door of the chopper as it lifted up, swirling and firing, his partner dangling from the end of his other arm. A team member reached down and grabbed the guy at the end of Buckman's arm, pulling him in. Buckman rolled himself into the centre of the chopper. He lay on the chopper floor, panting. The envoy was crying. They were giving medical attention to the injured team members. Buckman reached down his leg and felt blood. He pulled back his pant leg and saw that his stiletto was disfigured. It had deflected a bullet for him. The prime minister never forgot the incident or the bravery. Buckman advanced quickly in the agency.

"Excuse me, sir?"

Buckman opened his eyes.

"Would you like some peanuts and a soft drink?" asked the flight attendant.

"Ginger ale, please," he said, smiling as he reached out to take the drink and peanuts.

He opened the bag and popped a few nuts into his mouth. He looked out his window into the soft fluffiness of the clouds. He thought of Mac. She had agreed to meet him in Vegas. She would be arriving on Saturday. He hadn't told her about his other objective for being in Vegas. He could observe and be with Mac at the same time. She didn't need to know. Not yet. He didn't know when they would have a chance to be together again. He didn't want to miss this opportunity.

He listened to the hum of the aircraft's engines and looked out his window. At least at that extraction mission, he had known his target. This time, he had no idea. It was going to be a long weekend. He finished his ginger ale, pulled down the blind on his window, leaned back, and closed his eyes.

CHAPTER THREE

FRIDAY, MAY 22 | EVENING | ITALY

The Canadian Security Advisor (SA) unlocked the door to her room in Hotel Villa Clementina near Lake Braccinno to the north of Rome. She walked in and dropped her briefcase and light mauve jacket on the bed. She turned and went back into the small hall, locked her door, and walked to the room beside her, knocked on the door, and waited impatiently for an answer.

The door opened and a tall, handsome man with a small goatee stood to one side as she entered. Two glasses of wine were already poured and waiting on a table on the small balcony, as were two chairs. She went over, lifted a glass, drew the aroma into her nose, and closed her eyes in appreciation. With her eyes still closed, the man came over, stood behind her, and put his arms around her waist, nuzzling her neck with his nose before he began to kiss her neck, moving to her shoulder. He moved the strap of her bra out of the way in order to keep kissing her skin.

"You smell as good as the wine," he said in a strong French accent.

She smiled, sipping the wine, then turning her lips to meet his.

"The wine tastes so much better off your lips," he crooned.

"It's wonderful wine, as always. Thank you. It is

exactly what I needed."

"Just the wine?" And he pushed what was below his belt buckle against her hip. She turned to kiss him again.

"For now, yes." She took a long sip from the glass and placed it on the table, beginning to pace across the room. "Things don't feel right anymore."

"*D'accord*. Someone is holding out on us."

"I don't like that Kitch is involved and that we have threatened his life. It was never supposed to be like this. We wanted to change things."

"We still can. It is a small, how you say, hiccup."

"A pretty big hiccup. Why hasn't anyone pressed to find out who ordered that hit on Ian?"

"We can pursue that later. Right now, we have to stay on course. We have created a very tight timeline for all this."

"Two years ago, you and I met at a government conference. We were both infuriated by the human rights violations in China, and yet they continued to dictate terms to the world. Everyone turned a blind eye, afraid to impose serious sanctions. They were literally getting away with murder. Do you remember?"

"*Bien sûr*, of course I do. We were all concerned that our elected officials were becoming mere pawns to China and were growing more and more concerned about where that would lead."

"So, you convinced me and a few other advisors that something must be done, and we were the ones to do it. That we could form an alliance and take power of our countries and close the doors to China and put a stop to their spread of diseases and dictatorship. And soon more countries would follow."

"We feared for democracy."

"Exactly. Our goal was to bring democracy back to life. And then we brought in Ian, who basically created the plan that would put us into positions of power. He totally agreed with our agenda."

"Oui. Mais quelque chose s'est passe."

"Yes, that is exactly the question. Someone on the Strike Force has gone rogue. I'm sure of it. They ordered the hit on Ian. But why? And why now, when we are so close to our goal?"

"It is not a question to ask now. The question is: do we want to go forward? Do we want to put China in its place and take leadership? Do we want to save democracy?"

"Power is a dangerous drug. Maybe we are all getting drunk on it. Do we want to continue? Do *I* want to continue?"

She turned and sat down in one of the chairs on the balcony, picking up the glass of wine, sipping, and looking at the view. He sat down opposite her and lifted his glass, looking at her.

"Beautiful."

"Yes, it really is," she said, admiring the mountains bathed in the setting sun. "Worth saving. Worth preserving."

"I totally agree," he said.

She turned and looked at him. "Yes. To answer your question, yes, we go forward. I want to go forward. Some things are bigger than one person."

"And the person responsible will be discovered at the right time."

"Hopefully not at our expense," she said.

He put down his glass, stood up, and reached for hers, taking it and putting it beside his on the table. He extended his hand, and she placed her fingers in his palm. He drew her to her feet and pulled her into his arms, then spun her around in a few dance steps until they were sitting on the edge of the bed. He pulled the strap off her shoulder and began to kiss her again.

"And now to what you really needed when you walked into my room," he said.

She laughed, turning to kiss him, and began unbuttoning his shirt as his hands slid up inside hers.

SATURDAY, MAY 23 | USA

Las Vegas. Not what one would call a subtle and quiet city. More a glitzy oasis in the middle of the desert where organized crime comes home to roost. Where lives are broken and dreams come true. Where you can get divorced fast and married even faster. The only constant in Las Vegas was change, and best to be on the correct side of that change.

Cole stood still in the early evening outside the Bellagio hotel as the lights and sounds whirled around him. Early in Vegas was about 8:00 p.m. He made mental notes of the people passing by: what they were wearing, distinguishing features, anomalies, a pleasant energy or one that prickled his skin. Nothing stood out he needed to be wary of. He turned to watch the fountain with his arms around Mac. The fountain was one of her favourite places. She loved Vegas. She loved the thrill, the energy, the risk, the reward. And he loved to watch her. He never got tired of it.

They had got an early 1:00 p.m. check-in at the Bellagio and had agreed to meet in their room on the twelfth floor. The room was reserved for Mr. and Mrs. Boss. They both didn't arrive until after three o'clock in the afternoon. Mac lounged in the sheets on one of the queen beds, having pulled back the checkered duvet cover.

She wore a small white flower behind one ear. A bottle of opened water sat on the nightstand. She'd left the checkered curtains that matched the bedspread open to allow for natural light. The television in the console played a soft playlist of nondescript music. Her suitcase and clothes were tossed onto the other queen bed in the room. After a long three years, they didn't waste any time with small talk.

Cole dropped all his gear on the bed, stripped out of his clothes like they were on fire, and slid onto the sheet beside Mac. Their bodies talked loudly; skin on skin, breathless anticipation, tongues and lips, fingers in hair, limbs intertwined. There wasn't a sheet left on the bed when they finished, hours later, after many body conversations. And then there was nothing left for their bodies to say, for the moment anyway.

"I'm hungry," said Cole.

"I'm starving," said Mac, her finger drawing circles on his chest. "Plus," she said, climbing out of the bed, turning and looking at Cole, "I want to get to those slot machines." He looked at her standing there, craving her again, and reached for her hand, pulling her back onto the bed. He didn't want to get dressed just yet.

"We could just order room service," he said.

"We could, but it would be really hard to put one of those slot machines on the food cart." She smiled and kissed him before looking at the time showing on his cell phone screen. "Holy shit, it's 7:00 p.m. No wonder we're hungry."

"Best workout in the world," said Cole.

"Yeah, a four-hour workout; of course, that includes the napping. I'm super starving. Come on, take me to my favourite place, we'll get something to eat, work a few slots, and then we'll come back and take all our clothes off again."

"Deal," he said, kissing her fingers. It had been a ravishing afternoon. They showered together, which led to more body talk, and finally they were dressed and walking toward the elevator. They made their way to Mac's favourite spot. Cole pulled her close to him, the spray from the fountain falling close to their feet. He nibbled at her ear.

"Ready for that food?" she asked. "Let's find a table where we can still see the fountain. I could watch it all night."

"I know just the table," said Cole. Their hands slipped together, and they walked back into the Bellagio, passing an ice cream shop. "Dessert later?" he asked, pointing to the cones.

"Yummy," said Mac. "Or we could start eating them here and finish them with no clothes on in the room. I'd love to find out how butterscotch ripple ice cream tastes *à la* Cole."

Cole stopped dead in his tracks, pulled her over to him, and kissed her hard. "Can't wait for dessert," he said.

They made their way over to the escalator and rode it up to the casino floor. As they walked down the hallway, four people came out of the service entrance pushing two large garbage bins. Cole slowed down the sound and movement in the hall. They were dressed in brown coveralls with brown caps pulled low on their foreheads. He assessed each body type and weight, gender, eye movement. He scanned the clothes for places where weapons would hide. He felt his skin chill slightly.

As they passed each other, one of the women lifted her hand to adjust her cap, and Mac noticed a small serpent tattoo on her inner wrist. An image flashed across Mac's mind, but at the same time, Cole had put his arm around her waist and pulled her close, whispering in her ear. She lost the image.

"How about a table in the balcony here? We can still see the fountain, and the slots aren't far away." Cole turned to watch where the four in brown were heading, but they were gone.

"Beautiful. Super quiet isn't it? Kind of weird," said Mac.

"Everyone is in the bar at the other end, watching the pre-fight. The big fight is coming up soon. There are big-screen TVs all over Vegas tonight. Everyone will be watching the fight." He thought about the four in the hall again.

"Perfect, less people on slot machines, and we'll get our food faster. Why don't you get us a table. I am going to play the slots for a couple of minutes. I have twenty bucks to get rid of."

"Shall I order for you?"

"Sure. Glass of red. Salad. And I'll have a couple of slices of your pizza."

"How do you know I'm going to order pizza?"

"Four-hour workout? You're ordering a Hawaiian pizza."

"Okay, miss smarty pants, and what am I drinking?"

"Well, you'll start with a Jack on the rocks and then have a pint of draft with the pizza." She laughed, kissed him, and walked over to the slot machines.

Cole smiled and shook his head as he walked over to the hostess to get a table. Mac was so fucking sexy. And so fucking sharp. That made her irresistible. He walked to the balcony bar area to get a table, which wouldn't be much of a problem while the fights were happening.

While Mac fed a slot machine and Cole procured the perfect table, about sixty-five metres away in the money cage, four people wearing masks, brown clothes, and caps worked fast. They knew they had nine minutes to complete the job, one minute in the cage. They all pulled their weapons and tools from the bins. DangPa burst into the cage and quickly shot the two security guards and three staff squarely in the chest with her small beanbag rifle, causing immediate blunt force trauma and little noise. To seal the deal, Dagger whacked the one security guard in the head with the butt of his rifle and Berea choked out the second guard. Cobra was already zip-tying their hands behind their backs and putting duct tape over their mouths before they could breathe again and scream. DangPa helped her. While the two zip-tied and gagged the victims, Dagger and Berea stuffed the money from the cage, the fight-night money, into their knapsacks. When finished, they all worked to put bags over the heads of their victims. They would remember little when they woke up.

"One minute, *GO*," directed Dagger.

They quickly wiped down the disposable weapons, packed them back into the bins, adjusted their masks and Glocks in their holsters, and pulled out two large banners. They were now running out from behind the cash office.

"Seven minutes left, *GO*," said Dagger.

As Mac put a coin into a machine, a movement caught her eye and she looked up. She saw the brown outfits, the bins, the masks. She squinted to make out the masks: headshots of the fighters that night, Anthony Johnson and Daniel Cormier. Something didn't feel right. Her years as an intelligence officer told her these guys were up to no good.

"Cole," yelled Mac, already up and running across the room. Military training became second nature. If a threat was sensed, action was needed. Mac acted. But as she approached, the assailants stretched out the two large banners, each as long as a stretched limo and as wide as a car door. They lifted them high, each one holding an end, and started to run, like they were trying to launch a kite. Mac noticed that one of them had torn the glove on the left hand; she was close enough to see there was a missing middle finger.

The banners promoted the fight and the fighters that night. The assailants started running through the building. As they ran past casino guests, they got high-fives and thumbs up as everyone was excited and fired up about the big fight event. People started cheering, encouraging them, standing to watch. They started chanting the names of the fighters, their masks and banners egging the crowd on. Cole and Mac chased behind, looking to alert security, trying to dodge people moving around to see the banners and the masks.

The banners kept moving into the lobby. The cheering got louder and the sounds followed them as they exited the building, dropped the banners, and dove into a black Chevy Suburban, one of seven identical vehicles parked outside the doors. The Suburban started rolling down the ramp, headed out onto the strip, and disappeared.

Mac and Cole stood outside the doors, breathless. Security guards had followed them out. They all stood watching the SUVs pull away. The security detail called it in. Cole picked up the banners and looked at them, then he looked at Mac.

"Not much more we can do here," he said.

"Security will deal with it now, if there's anything to deal with," she said.

"Oh, I'm sure there is, but sometimes it's not my problem."

"I do like that you can make that kind of decision, Mr. Boss."

Cole smiled. "Think the pizza will be ready?"

"I sure as fuck hope the glass of wine is."

They turned and headed back up to their table, arm in arm. Their food was waiting for them when they arrived and sat down. They both lifted their drinks and clinked them together.

"Cheers."

"What did you see?" asked Cole, lifting up a pizza slice.

"So much for it not being your problem," said Mac.

"Well, I'm not chasing them, am I? Just curious is all."

Mac smiled, picking up a slice of his pizza. She took her time chewing and swallowing, sipping her wine, and then started to talk.

While Mac explained about the torn glove and missing finger, the black Suburban the Cell had jumped into careened through the city, heading out into the pitch-dark of the desert. Sirens started fading behind them. Berea sat beside the driver. He reached over and grabbed the steering wheel at the same moment Cobra shot the driver in the head from the back seat. Dagger leaned over the back seat, opened the driver's door, and pushed the corpse onto the road. Berea deftly slid into the driver's seat.

"I thought they said no more killing," said DangPa.

"So we don't tell them," said Berea.

"How much?" asked Cobra.

"About five mil," said Dagger.

"They were hoping for more," said Cobra.

"That means one more job," said Berea.

"I already reserved the jet for midnight, just in case."

"Flight plan?"

"Atlantic City."

They all nodded.

"How far to the other vehicle?"

"Just up ahead," said Berea.

They pulled up to an abandoned gas station. They climbed out of the Suburban, leaving their brown coveralls and caps in the back seat, and hopped into the waiting silver Ford Taurus. They turned back toward the motel where their weapons waited, packed and ready for the next assignment.

Meanwhile, Cole had ordered his draft and was on his last slice of pizza. Mac had decided on a pint herself rather than more wine. She had enjoyed a slice of Cole's pizza. He didn't mind sharing his food with her.

"No wonder you're in intel, Mac; you have a keen eye. Where do you know that tattoo from again?"

"Before I worked Intel, I did a job on the ground. She was one of my team members."

"But lots of people could have that tattoo on their wrist."

"But not lots of people would have part of their middle finger missing on the same hand."

Cole nodded, his mouth full. "Go on," he said, putting the food to one side of his mouth.

"She had great skill but a bad attitude. Not a team player at all. Almost cost the lives of the team. We weren't unhappy when she was transferred out. I was moved into intel shortly after. That's where I heard she'd deserted."

"And the finger?"

"That was a freak accident. She was working with a piece of machinery at the base, and her hand got caught. She was lucky she didn't lose her whole hand. Pissed her off, though. Said it would throw off her marksmanship."

"Well, she was pretty slick tonight. They all were."

"Is that the other reason you were here?"

"Mac, I'm hurt. I was here for you."

"Cole, I'm intel for a reason."

"Can't tell you, not yet. But I may need your help."

"Of course you will." She winked at him. "Want to help me get that butterscotch ice cream to go, right about now?"

"You read my mind."

CHAPTER FOUR

SUNDAY, MAY 24 | CANADA

Kitch sat in his condo nursing a Scotch and his wounds, emotional and physical. He was scared. He knew he couldn't interpret or continue Ian's work. He could barely navigate his cell phone. Even the thought of delving into the deep, dark depths of technology could give him a panic attack. Especially when there was a gun to the back of his head, as he now knew there was. All he had done a few years ago was recommend Ian when the security advisor to the Canadian PM had asked for a name. Someone Kitch trusted in computer technology and had a background in undercover work. Ian's name had come to mind instantly. Colin's was a backup name. It didn't seem an odd request at the time. The government was always dealing in closed-door discussions, and technology was having a greater role all the time. Having worked with the IRA for a number of years, he knew Ian was versed in working on the QT, and his computer skills were unparalleled. And he said Colin was basically his mentor. That was it. Kitch had given the names and thought no more of it. When he hadn't heard from Ian, he wasn't even sure if he had taken the job. Or maybe Colin had. He hadn't had time to give it much thought. Then Ian showed up in the courtroom, wasn't giving his identity, and Kitch knew something was wrong. That's why he tried to get to him quickly after the trial. To find out what was going on. Then the shooting happened, the hospital, the ICU, a suited man at the end of his bed, and then being summoned to Italy without a choice. He had to think. He had to think. He refilled his glass.

While Kitch sat thinking in his condo, his son was thinking out loud with his Wookies on *Windy Girl*.

"It sounds like you found what you went looking for," said Anderson.

"Excellent intel, by the way, Anderson," said Foster.

Anderson smiled.

"So you went looking for this crew that took a private jet to Vegas and basically caught them with their hand in the cookie jar," said Harrod.

"Literally," said Thornton.

"Why didn't you intervene?" asked Harrod.

"It all happened so fast. I wasn't even expecting them to be there. I was thinking I'd track them down the next day. I was getting a table for Mac and I to have dinner…"

"A little work combined with pleasure," said Foster, "you dog. Care to share any details?"

"Let's just say that butterscotch ripple ice cream melts quickly on skin and is rather sticky." Buckman winked.

They all laughed and high-fived; Anderson rolled her eyes.

"But seriously, I couldn't intervene. I didn't even see

the job at first; Mac did. By that time, they had moved into the second half of the operation. It was clever. Really clever. They're smooth. I stood and took mental notes."

"And?" asked Anderson.

"Four. Two were tall and muscular, another about 5'10" and solid, one slight but agile. Couldn't see their faces, but one had a ripped glove and Mac saw that there was a finger missing on the left hand."

"And you figured these were the same four that came out of the service door earlier and there was a tattoo on an inside wrist, correct?" said Foster.

"Yes, but Mac said the tattoo and the finger are on the same hand, on the same person," said Buckman.

"Wait a minute. A finger off the left hand and a serpent tattoo. Combine that with the info I discovered about the button Foster found at the scene of the shooting by the courthouse, and I think we have identified one of that Cell."

"Do tell," said Foster.

"Sarah Thompson."

"And…" pushed Anderson.

"Okay, I trained recruits to the special forces for a few years. There was a woman then, fantastic sniper. Had a real edge, which could serve a sniper well. Also had a real attitude. Turns out that attitude was her downfall," said Harrod.

"Yeah, Mac said the same thing. That she'd worked with her before going into intel, and she was not a team player," said Buckman.

"Guess she just needed to find her team," said Thornton. Every eye slowly turned and looked at him. "Sorry," he said.

"Thornton's right," said Harrod. "She did need to find her team. Apparently, she has. Now it all makes sense. She earned one of those coveted shirts from the special forces. Meant a lot to her. Wore it when she wasn't supposed to. I did hear she had lost a finger in a freak accident, not even on a mission. Got her serpent tattoo shortly after. Then she went MIA. Can easily imagine she wore that same shirt during that shooting job in Toronto. And here's another thing: she had a serious hard-on for one specific weapon; the FNAB-43 submachine gun."

"Isn't that the projectile you found from that weapon?" asked Anderson.

"Bingo was his name-o," sang Harrod.

"And there weren't many of that weapon made, few still in use," said Foster.

"So Sarah Thompson is definitely one of that mercenary Cell," said Buckman.

"Without a doubt," said Harrod.

"So the next question is, who are they working for?" said Thornton.

"And who are the others on the team?" said Foster.

"Are you going to sing Bingo again?" asked Anderson.

"I was thinking we could do a little round together," said Harrod.

"Okay, this is going to require some deep, dark work to get us started," said Anderson. "I'm going to reach out to my computer trainer at Quantico. See if he has any suggestions I haven't thought of."

"Foster?" Cole prompted.

"Going to talk to some guys at the station. See if I can find out anything more about our guy, Ian."

"I'll see if Sarah has popped up on a grid anywhere in the last while. Look into that button a bit further, and the weapon," said Harrod.

"I'm going to see if Mac has any more details on when and where Sarah got that tattoo. Maybe something there," said Buckman.

"That all sounds perfect. There's a southwester blowing in. I think I'll give *Windy Girl* a run. Stretch her legs a little," said Thornton.

"Just make sure it's gentle stretching, Thornton. I don't want to be hurling all over my new equipment," said Anderson.

MONDAY, MAY 25 | USA, CANADA, FRANCE, BRITAIN, ITALY

Through parts of Europe and North America, a clandestine feat of digital engineering was underway, all designed and orchestrated by Ian Duncan. The agenda of the Strike Force was being implemented, flooding the Internet with untraceable whisper messages, creating doubt, questions, and concerns in the minds of citizens about their leaders.

Facebook posts were popping onto random screens while citizens sat with their morning coffee, scrolling through their social media feeds. That morning, the focus of varied posts was racist activities. And the activities were vaguely linked to leaders in the G8 countries. Ian had created a program that randomly replied to these posts, further implicating the leaders in these unsavoury actions. People read the comments, believing them to be true, and felt more and more uncomfortable. They began sending messages to their own friends, asking if they had seen this post, sharing it, and the conversations began. The smear began to spread like a virus.

Texts, tweets, Facebook replies, and comments began surging through people's devices, tarnishing current leaders and pointing to an alternative soon to be announced. It was all very cloak-and-dagger, but that was Ian's goal. He wanted to pique curiosity, garner attention, interest, intrigue, yearning in everyone who turned on their device and went in search of stories. And then, at just the right moment of chaos, the name of the heroic reformer and saviour would be announced, one for each country.

It was the first shining moment for the Strike Force. The next phase of their agenda would take place in ten days, as meticulously laid out by Ian. But someone had to implement the last key pieces. They didn't have to design it; they just had to carry it out. Kitch would have to find someone in time. As each member sat in front of a computer screen watching the mayhem unfold, they hoped their threat to Kitch had been enough motivation.

One member leaned back in his recliner chair, puffing on his cigarette, watching his screen in his living room. He would let it all play out. It was out of his hands. He knew that Ian had discovered his double-cross. He wasn't sure if Ian knew his reasons. But before everything could be ruined, he had taken him out. His sister's life was at stake. She had been doing humanitarian work in China and had been arrested. It was never clear why. China never had to give a reason for any arrests they made. Shortly after, he had received a very threatening message. They had found out about the Strike Force. He had no idea how. They had been so incredibly careful. Ian had been a master at disguise. It had been a lofty goal to find a way to give countries more leverage and so reduce China's threat of global infiltration. With new leaders in place, they could begin to implement new policies and stop sharing labs and technology with China, only to have that information abused and misused. The Strike Force had lists of what could be done to take back power for governments that promoted true freedom.

But China's computer surveillance systems were without measure and clearly not only within their own great walls. They wanted the agenda of the Strike Force stopped, quietly, and were using his sister as insurance. He thought taking out Ian would be enough for it all to crumble. He had underestimated the Strike Force.

MONDAY, MAY 25 | USA

Ab Kipley at Quantico in Virginia pushed papers aside on his desk and pulled his laptop forward. His fingers hovered over the keys as he pondered his entry. He had been instructing the fine art of computer hacking, surveillance, and anything dark and mysterious on the Internet for over ten years. His covert op days were long behind him. The Rolex glittering on his left wrist was the last gift he had received on assignment, although from whom and for what reason he would tell no one. He was short and balding, a little roly-poly. Definitely the kind of guy kicked out of bed for eating crackers, if he was invited to your bed at all. But invited to your computer? That was a totally different ballgame. Ab was a genius. And his students were top of their game. The cell phone to his right reflected his rectangular black-rimmed bifocals as he picked it up to see who was calling. It was one of the secure numbers he had assigned to his students. He was always there if they needed him, only a call away. Ab Kipley wasn't a bullshitter.

He clicked the speaker icon and started to talk. "Ms. Anderson, to what do I owe this unique pleasure of speaking with you?"

Anderson laughed. "Thanks, Ab. How are things at your end?"

"Same old, same old. Any juicy tidbits from the sordid world for me?"

"Not sure. Probably. You know how it is."

"I do indeed. What is stumping you?"

"I have a feeling this case is going to delve into new areas of the dark web and beyond. I haven't gone beyond in a while. Hoping you could bring me up to speed and point me in the right direction."

"Ahhh, the dark web. Yes, she does hold her secrets close to her heart. The world of deep, dark whispers is becoming the new order, it would appear. In the last few days…"

Ab went on to explain what he had discovered about how to enter the world of compromise, and he and Anderson spoke at length. She was satisfied that she now had the tools she would need to get what she wanted.

"Kitch still doing well since his surgery? He seemed like he was doing fine a few days ago." asked Ab.

It didn't surprise Anderson that he knew or was asking. It was a close world they both worked in, and they kept tabs on people they had worked with. Ab knew Anderson had ties to Kitch and his son. Plus Ab knew everything and anything that anyone was doing.

"He recovered from his surgery and left the hospital ahead of schedule," said Anderson, withholding the information about his travelling to Italy, and not asking why he was talking with Kitch. She knew better.

"Yes, well that sounds about right. He called me just the other day, asking a question very similar to yours, in fact, although a bit more specific."

Anderson didn't register her surprise. She replied calmly. "Well, Kitch is always digging into something, I guess."

"Yes, that is true. Well, if you happen to cross paths, give him my best. And if you need anything else my dear, never hesitate to call. Always lovely to talk with you."

"Thanks, Ab. You take care."

"And you, Anderson."

Anderson hung up and leaned back in her chair. They had stepped into a tangled web, and not just online. What was going on? She had to talk to Buckman, and fast. She dialled his number.

"Cole?"

"Correct."

"It's time to go fishing."

"Target?"

"Your dad."

TUESDAY, MAY 26 | MORNING | CANADA

Cole thought about the conversation with Trish a hundred times. He was surprised his dad was keeping such a secret. Something was off. He rolled what Trish had told him around in his brain, over his tongue, and through his fingers as he cleaned his gun. Cleaning his weapon was a methodical process. It allowed him to focus his thoughts. He carefully put the cleaning rods, jags, and lubricants back into their container. He locked the gun back together and slipped it into his holster. With all that was going on, he felt a weapon on his hip might come in handy. He wiped off the counter and stood in the kitchen as he drank a glass of water. He had to talk to his dad. He put the empty glass into the sink and grabbed his keys.

Down on the street, he hailed a cab and soon stood outside his dad's building. He took the elevator up, walked down the hall, and knocked on the door. His dad didn't know he was coming. Cole didn't even know if he would be there. He stood to the side of the door so if Kitch looked through the peephole, he would see no one. He'd have to call out or open the door. He hoped for the call out. He'd be able to tell by sound of his dad's voice if he was alone.

"Who's there?"

Cole heard the worry, the hesitation in his voice.

That's what he had needed to hear. Because if there hadn't been some fear, there was a greater chance he was involved. He also knew he was alone. He decided on his next course of action. He moved in front of the peephole.

"Hi, Dad," he said.

The door opened. Kitch walked away as Cole stepped inside, closing and locking the door behind him. He followed Kitch over to the sitting area, stopping to turn on some loud music just in case the place was bugged. They sat and looked at each other in silence for what seemed like hours.

"How are you feeling?" asked Cole, easing his way inside a deeper conversation.

"Tired," said Kitch.

Well, flying halfway across the world and back in two days after major surgery will do that to ya, thought Cole. "Surgery can take a toll on the body, Dad."

Kitch still hadn't looked Cole in the eye.

"Can I get you something?"

Kitch looked up at that question. Right into Cole's eyes. He spoke softly. "Son, do you remember what your mother used to do if you were keeping a secret, or I was keeping a secret?"

"Sure I do, she'd sing "My Favourite Things." So corny." He smiled warmly though.

"And after the song?"

"She'd ask if she could get me something: mittens, a kettle, a truth serum. And she'd laugh and kiss me on the cheek. Always made me feel so good, all that corny stuff, I just felt safe to tell her everything. Did she do that to you too?"

"Almost exactly."

They sat in silence again, eyes locked on each other.

"Dad?"

"Yes."

"We may both need a stiff drink if I start to sing "My Favourite Things," but can I get you some mittens, a kettle, a truth serum?" And Cole proceeded to get up, walk over to his dad, sit down beside him, and put his arm around him. His dad leaned forward and put his head into his hands.

"I'm in over my head, Cole," he barely whispered. "I have no idea how it happened, but I'm fucked."

"Are you inside or outside?"

Kitch sat up and turned slowly to face Cole. He knew eye contact at that moment was imperative. Especially talking with his son. "Completely outside."

"Then before you say another word, grab your coat. Let's go."

Kitch went to turn off the music. Cole shook his head. They both left the apartment, music a bit louder than before.

As they exited Kitch's building, Cole alerted the

Wookies to meet immediately at Control Center. He waved for a cab. *These fuckers need to have my stiletto blade stuck into their carotid artery*, thought Cole. *No square-bashing, no drill.*

TUESDAY, MAY 26 | MORNING | BRITAIN

Inside the prime minister's office, employees were being flooded with emails, calls, texts, tweets.

"How on earth did this information get out there?"

"Absolutely no idea."

"Where are all these Facebook posts originating? These answers are inciting paranoia."

"Clearly the goal is to discredit the PM."

"No shit, Sherlock. But why? These comments aren't about policy; they're about things said years ago."

"Look at this email. That 'thing' said years ago is being spun to be relevant now."

"But it isn't."

"Well, it is now."

"These are all personal texts. They're sending copies. These aren't robocall issues; these are direct messages."

"Which means people are opening them."

"And reading them."

"And believing them."

"Which means…"

"We have a problem."

"Did you see this? Looks like someone else close to the PM is being set up as the saviour." Everyone gathered around that desk, bent down, and peered at the screen. They all stood up in unison.

"Who is it?"

"*To be named at the appropriate time,* that's what it says at the bottom here."

"Fuck."

"Hang on, it's not just here. This is happening in other countries as well."

"Holy fuck."

"Doesn't really matter. The damage is already being done here."

"Yeah, that's right. Once a voter works with a seed of doubt, it's hard to shift that thinking."

"Not impossible, though."

"Here, I did a cross-reference to this one tiny post. All the people that received this love to golf."

"And our PM hates it."

"What the hell is going on?"

"This is more than a smear campaign."

"Think Secret Intelligence Service knows?"

"Well, if they don't, they should all be fired."

"Maybe they're not getting these social media messages. Maybe they're off 'the list.'"

"Maybe, but I'm going to make a few calls."

"I'm going to reach out to a few other countries, see what they've noticed."

"I don't think we're going home for a while."

"Well, pull out that bottle you have tucked in your

bottom drawer."

"Already pouring."

"I'm calling the security advisor to the PM."

The phone rang in the posh flat in Clarendon Cross. The security advisor rarely arose at such an early hour. She wrapped a robe around her thin nightgown and made her way into the large living room, bathed in morning light through a wall of ceiling to floor windows. She glanced at the coffee maker on her counter, which was programmed to begin brewing momentarily. She sat on the couch and answered the phone.

"Yes?"

"Sorry to bother you at this hour, ma'am, but we have a problem we feel you need to be aware of."

"Continue."

"It seems that social media is being inundated with slanderous messages about the prime minister."

"Direct slander?"

"No, not exactly. Very thin connections, but people are buying into it. It is like a smear campaign using current crime waves, past indiscretions. I've actually never seen anything quite like it before."

The SA got up and went to the kitchen, waiting for her coffee, a small smile on her face. "Thank you for the brief. Have your people send me details to my secure email. I'll review this afternoon and get back to you."

"Very good, ma'am."

The SA poured herself a coffee. She took the mug of black energy and went back to the couch. She leaned against the pillows, sipping from her cup. The plan was working. Ian had been a genius. Soon China wouldn't be able to play by its own rules anymore. The Strike Force would put an end to its impending international order and authoritarian control. *Soon we will have leaders who refuse to capitulate.*

She put down her coffee and began to detail a note to members of the Strike Force. She wanted to know if their countries were experiencing the same force of Ian's plan.

TUESDAY, MAY 26 | AFTERNOON | CANADA

They all sat around the table below deck on the *Windy Girl*. Kitch looked drawn, haggard, with dark circles under his eyes.

"Good to see ya, man," said Harrod.

"You're looking good," said Thornton.

"Fuck off," said Kitch. "I look like shit."

"He does," said Foster.

"I was trying to be nice," said Thornton.

"How can we help?" said Anderson. "We got together to find out who shot you."

"Yeah, Cole told me. I don't know what to say."

"Just say it's not going to happen again," said Harrod.

"Can't say that, not now."

"Walk us through it, buddy," said Thornton.

Cole sat back, watching, listening. He said nothing and let his team take over.

Kitch took a deep breath. "Any Scotch on this vessel?"

Thornton got up and poured him a shot. "Anyone else?" They waved him to sit down.

"A couple of years ago, the security advisor to our PM asked me for a name," Kitch said.

"Why?" asked Thornton.

"I didn't ask."

"First mistake," said Foster.

"Yeah. But it wasn't out of the ordinary. I'd done a lot of work for her here and there in court, out of court in a legal advisor fashion, so when she asked me for a name of someone I trusted, someone well versed in computers and covert ops, I immediately thought of Ian. And as a backup, a friend of his, Colin. Didn't think any more of it. I mean, we go back, we worked together in the Crown's office when we first got into this legal business." He snorted at the irony and took a drink.

"How did you know Ian?" asked Anderson.

"We went way back too. I was negotiating with the IRA overseas; Ian was on their side of the table. We hit it off, grabbed some pints together, and stayed in touch. Nothing more than that, really. Grabbed a drink here and there when we were in the same country. Good guy. Always said he was with the IRA to stop corrupt governments. He felt the world was spiralling toward a time when the elected leader would just be a puppet to larger corruption. He wanted that to change."

"And he thought the IRA was doing that," said Harrod.

"Well, it was, in a way, back then anyway. And it did make people stop and think. After that he realized technology was the future of everything, so he became an expert."

"He wasn't wrong about that either," said Anderson.

"He was a brilliant guy. Good heart too. Anyway, I gave his name, and Colin's, and that was it. Didn't even hear if he'd taken the job, didn't even know what the job was, until…"

"Until you saw him in court that day," said Cole.

"Exactly. I couldn't understand why he wasn't giving his identity. He was never the anonymous type. And he wouldn't even look at me. I knew something was up, so I played along, figured I'd get to him as he walked out to the paddy wagon…"

"But I was there, slowed things down."

"Yeah. But what would you have thought if I'd just blown you off? I couldn't do that. And there was no time to explain. So, I tried to be quick and then ran after him."

"But he was already outside," said Foster.

"And that's when the shooting started," said Harrod.

"And you never got to ask him what was going on," said Anderson.

"Exactly." Kitch took a drink.

"Why were you on a plane to Italy so soon after your surgery? You'd taken a lot of bullets," said Anderson.

Kitch's eyes widened like he'd been given a shot of adrenaline, and he looked at Anderson.

"We were worried about you. I had a cyber track on you," said Anderson.

Kitch took a bigger swig.

Thornton got up, grabbed the bottle, and put it in front of him.

"I was summoned," said Kitch.

They all looked at each other. "By whom?" they asked simultaneously.

"That's the thing, and where it gets a bit chilly. I have no idea."

"Absolutely no idea?" asked Thornton.

"None," said Kitch.

"When you got there?" asked Foster.

"Nope, then it got ice-cold." He took another drink. "I was picked up at the airport in Italy by this heavy-set guy in an immaculate suit. He looked familiar. And then I remembered that there had been a guy standing at the end of my bed when I was in ICU. Never talked to me. Just stood there. I was so drugged up, he blurred in and out of my vision, and then he was gone."

"I remember that guy," said Cole. "He was getting on the elevator when I was getting off. Agitated. I knew something was off, but I didn't get any other vibe off him. Put it down to him visiting someone in ICU."

"That's because he's a nobody. Just a messenger, a driver. No vibe to pick up. Anyway, he puts me in the back of the sedan and handcuffs me and hoods me."

"What the fuck?" said Harrod.

"That's what I was thinking. We drove for about an hour, I'd guess. I was taken into a building, echoey…"

"So obviously empty, like a warehouse," said Cole.

"Yeah, maybe."

"Did you see them then?" asked Anderson.

"No, they never took off the hood."

Everyone looked at each other. They were starting to feel the same chill.

"I was put in a chair, and people started talking. I think I heard maybe five different voices. Hard to be certain under the circumstances. There were at least two women, and there were accents. I was traumatized and still in pain from the surgery. I don't remember everything that was said, but basically, because I gave them Ian's name…"

"So, he was working for them," said Foster.

"Not sure if it was for them, or with them."

Everyone sat very still.

"So we don't know why he was killed," said Harrod.

"Could have been part of his job, and something went wrong so they took him out," said Harrod.

"Or he didn't like something going on and was trying to get out," said Anderson.

"At that summit, when I caught him, he was either on assignment to deal with someone, or trying to warn someone, and that someone was the British PM," said Cole.

Thornton got up and pulled a glass off the shelf, came over, and poured himself a drink. "Anyone else?" Everyone put their hand up this time. He got glasses, put them on the table, and everyone poured. They sat and sipped, thinking.

"So, what did they say?"

"They called Ian their digital director, and because I gave his name, I am to take over his role. And if I can't do it, I have to find someone by Thursday."

"Or you join Ian," said Harrod.

"Yeah," said Kitch. "Some digital campaign has already been launched by Ian, and I have to implement part two, or this guy I find, that they have to approve, will finish the job."

"Big money?" asked Foster.

"Wouldn't say," said Kitch. "Said it would all be revealed to the person themselves; the money they'd pay and the assignment."

"Why don't they just ask another favour, another name, from someone else?"

"I think they're running out of time. They didn't expect to lose Ian. They need him, or at least that expertise."

"Well, we know it involves the dark web," said Anderson. "Ab told me himself." She turned and looked at Kitch.

"Fuck," he said.

"I spoke to Ab. He wanted me to say hello. Said you were asking questions similar to mine," said Anderson.

"You were?"

"The world works in dark ways, and technology is opening dangerous doors. I wanted some suggestions."

"It may become more than a suggestion," said Cole.

"What do you mean?" asked Anderson.

"I mean we have an 'in' to whatever is going on here. Obviously, we've stumbled into something bigger than any of us thought. And now we have to see it through, for many reasons," said Cole. They all took a drink, waiting. "Bill will be your IT guy, Dad. He'll go in undercover, which is what he does best, and Anderson will be his coach."

"It's perfect," said Foster.

"Bill? You okay with that?" Kitch asked.

"Absolutely. No one in this room is dying in the near future. Let's do this," said Thornton.

"Well, we already have a name," said Anderson. They all looked at her, heads tilted to one side, waiting. "Colin. Bill will be the other name Kitch gave. Simple."

"That's a great idea," said Cole. "Do you know where this guy is, Dad?"

"Not a clue. Never knew his last name. Tried to find him when I got back from Italy, but he's a real ghost.

There's not even a photo of him. Not anywhere."

"Like any good techie," said Anderson. "That makes it easier, actually. Especially if no one even knows what he looks like. We'll just make up a last name and create an identity. Easy-peasy."

Kitch refilled everyone's glass and bottomed his first. Nothing about this felt easy to him.

TUESDAY, MAY 26 | EVENING | FRANCE

One of the Strike Force members sat in front of his computer screen, a glass of exquisite Pinot Noir balanced in his hand. He loved the Napa wines, maybe because his ranch sat in the foothills of the Napa Valley. Walking out of his front door was like stepping into a dream. He was considering the email sent securely from the British SA. Yes, he had been alerted of similar activity on social media in his country. He sent a brief reply through their Virtual Private Network.

These updates were impressive. So much movement in such a short time. He sipped his wine. These Facebook posts and conversations were escalating. Now America's fearless leader's personality was being called into question. The waters were becoming muddy, and alternative exaggerated facts were becoming mainstream.

He leaned back in his chair. America and other countries had tried various strategies to reduce China's aggressive polices that threatened to reach beyond its own borders. China's military and economic strategies were making them more dangerous with each passing day. And he read just the other day that China was quietly buying up swathes of industrial assets throughout Europe. It seemed that only five people cared to stop the red giant.

He loved his country. He was not willing to sacrifice it

to cowardly policies with no vision. Soon he would be leader, and then China would be forced to take a back seat. Everything was moving ahead as Ian had prepared. But there was still the question as to why Ian was killed. He was so supportive of the work the Strike Force wanted to do. Had someone changed their minds? Their course? He couldn't believe it; they were all so committed. But something had gone wrong. He dearly hoped it would not compromise everything. There was too much at stake.

He reached for the bottle of Pinot Noir and refilled his wine goblet. He wondered if Kitch had found Ian's replacement. It would be unfortunate to have another casualty, but the war was being waged. There was no turning back.

He sent another secure message to the Strike Force. They needed to confirm that one more casino hit was in place. The expenses were mounting up: travel expenses, the database, the jet, and the list went on. Even though he was footing a lot of the bills, they needed one more increase in cash flow to get them to the election.

For now, the question of Ian's death would have to wait. He walked to the window, breathing in the mountain strength. He had a feeling he was going to need it.

WEDNESDAY, MAY 27 | CANADA

Kitch had sent the name of Ian's replacement to the Strike Force via the secure VPN address provided. He received word that there would be a call that evening on a secure line with Strike Force members, Kitch and Colin MacPherson, a.k.a. Bill Thornton, a.k.a. Doc. Kitch would be sent details an hour before the call via VPN.

The Wookies went into overdrive.

Cole sat and had Kitch relay his encounter with the Strike Force over and over again. He wanted to see if he could pick something out of his story that would help them going forward.

Foster was going to dig deeper into what the police knew about Ian. He thought he would pay Morty another visit and see if something had been missed.

Harrod was investigating the button from the shirt. He wanted to track down Sarah's last location.

Anderson was digging deep, very happy she had talked with Ab. He had shown her different ways of getting the information she would need, information for Thornton/Colin. She had a lot to try to get into his brain in a very short period of time. Of course, he'd be wearing an earpiece the whole time, so she could basically answer the questions for him, but experience had shown her that devices could fail. The undercover agent had to have a significant amount of info in their own brain, just in case.

Thornton was at the barber.

"Geez, man, you like a little girl who no wanna to lose her goldi-locks." The barber laughed out loud at Thornton's sulky face.

Thornton wasn't laughing. "Ah, Christ, I just hate the thought of having to shave every day. And actually brush my hair."

"Hey, I cut it so short, you no brush."

"Yeah, good."

"Everything off da face?"

"Nah, that's too financial district. Let's leave a small goatee."

"Sure, just a different sorta kitschy then."

Thornton rolled his eyes up to the barber. "Yeah, a different kind of kitschy," he said. *One that hopefully won't get me killed,* he thought.

One by one, Thornton's long, dark red, curly locks started falling to the floor. Soon, the chair was surrounded by hair, and the black nylon hair cape was littered with strands. The barber got his blow dryer and waved it over Thornton, clearing out the fallen hairs from his covering. Thornton ran his hand over his head.

"Okay?" said the barber.

"Okay," said Thornton.

The barber began to trim down Thornton's beard with

his clippers until the hairs were close to the face. Once again, the cape was covered in hair and the blow dryer was pulled out. Thornton glanced at his watch. Another reason he never cut his hair or beard; too much time wasted.

The barber went over to a sink and washed his hands, leaving them dripping wet. He came back, tapping the warm water onto Thornton's now short beard until his face was warm and soft. He dried his hands, squirted shaving cream into the cup of his palm, and dabbed it all over the beard. He then sharpened his blade, sliding it back and forth along his leather strop. The sound raised the hairs on the back of Thornton's neck. It took him back to an undercover job years ago. The criminal he was "buddies" with was sharpening a blade exactly the same way, but it wasn't going to be used to trim a beard. It was going to slice open the throat of the man tied in the chair. Thornton couldn't blow his cover. He stood, watching, and then had quietly reminded the criminal that if they killed this guy without the boss's okay, they would be next. He said to be smart. The guy slashed the victim's arm. Thornton had slowly walked over and taken the switchblade out of his hand. He told him to sit down while he questioned the guy. The guy tied up in the chair wasn't up for citizen of the year either, but Thornton wasn't going to have a murder on his watch, undercover or not. He maneuvered that situation and eventually brought down the whole ring, including the guy tied to the chair. He could never get that sound out of his head, though, the sharpening of a blade on a strop. Gave him the creeps. If he hadn't been there, that guy in the chair would have looked like a spaghetti dinner.

His attention came back to the barbershop. The blade slid smoothly over his face, revealing skin that hadn't been exposed in quite a few years. A fashionable goatee was shaped around his chin. When finished, the barber wiped the remaining cream off with a towel and patted a cool aftershave onto the skin.

Thornton turned his head from side to side, watching his reflection in the mirror. *Hi, Colin*, he said to himself. The makeover wasn't always for the client; it was so he could convince himself of his new role. He'd been out of the game for a bit. Now, he was ready. He stood up and slapped two twenties onto the guy's station.

"Thanks, man," he said.

And he was out the door, making his way back to *Windy Girl*.

WEDNESDAY, MAY 27 | USA

The Strike Force had contacted the Cell. They had been laying low outside Ocean City, N.J., letting the casino hit die down, waiting for their next assignment, and now they had it: they were to do one more hit at a casino in Atlantic City. It needed to be planned and timed in order to get the biggest withdrawal possible. They were told it would almost be their last job. If casualties were necessary, so be it. Mercenaries were hard to handle. Had to keep them on the hook until the absolute last second.

The Cell understood. They preferred it when they didn't have to worry about bodies. Made the job so much more straightforward. They began their research and planning.

WEDNESDAY, MAY 27 | AFTERNOON | CANADA

When Thornton climbed below the deck of the *Windy Girl*, Anderson turned around and did a double-take.

"Holy fuck," was all she could think to say. "Geek squad alert."

"Gee, thanks. I was hoping for something more debonair."

"Really? Wait till the others get here. I'm just warming you up."

"Fuck you," he said with a smile.

"Seriously, it's good. You're Colin now, and I'll start calling you that. Come have a look. I've been putting your profile together. It will be online in minutes. It has to be ready before your call later."

Thornton grabbed a beer from the small fridge and wheeled a small stool over beside Anderson. He could smell her shampoo. He put the beer to his lips, wishing instead the bottle could be her lips. He washed that thought down with more beer.

"Okay, Colin. First, let me take a photo." She reached over and grabbed her Canon Powershot G5 X camera. It was her go-to for easy high-quality photos that she could transfer online quickly. "Thornton, do you still have those reading glasses?"

"The bogus ones?"

"Yeah, I think they would make the geek persona complete." She gave him a wink.

He went and rustled around in his bunk area and came up with what she was hoping for. He put them on and posed for her.

"Sexy, baby." She laughed. "Okay, don't smile. Look sinister and intriguing and maybe a little stoned."

Thornton complied, and she snapped a few photos. She checked them out on the viewfinder. "Perfect," she said and started to put them onto her screen. She began to read her screen out loud to Thornton: "'Colin MacPherson. Competent, intensely focused, militant, gets the job done. After training at Quantico, he worked in the cyber-surveillance division of the FBI and CIA. Following that, he took his skills to groups looking for justice; IRA in Ireland and ETA in Spain and France. He currently works as a freelance technician.' What do you think?"

"Couldn't be better. Just brief me on the jobs I actually did," he said.

"Well, that's simple. You can't say and you won't say. Compromises your contacts and so credibility."

"Niiiice," he said.

"I've also set Colin up in an apartment in the Bloor West district."

"Nice restaurants there."

Trish stared at him. "There is also a black Honda

Accord in the parking lot registered to you."

"Excellent."

"So basically, this phone call will be your audition to save Kitch's life and uncover an international organization."

"Simple, no pressure at all." He rolled his eyes, widened them, and sucked back some beer.

"You up for this, sailor?"

"Sure, I've been out of the game for a while, but let's be honest, it's who I am. Am I up for it? Fucking right."

"Okay. I've done a lot of digging. Looks like Ian has set up a whole architecture of disinformation. It's brilliant, really. He even has what he calls digital code trolls that are doing his bidding and sending messages to unsuspecting citizens. Think of it as something like invisible radiation affecting anyone with a computer, cell phone, and tablet within his targeted areas. It doesn't appear to be worldwide. That I can't figure out just yet. Something for you to find."

"So, he's sort of cuddling up to citizens for a purpose and whispering in their ears."

"Exactly. What we don't know is the purpose of the whispering. I'm guessing he's put into place a database using psychographic targeting."

"So we're convincing people to think a certain way and then hope they'll do something with that information."

"Right. We just don't know what."

"Are they bending the truth or reinventing it?"

"Bit of both."

"What will step two be that I have to implement?"

"No clue. But this should give you enough background to be able to surf with them until they accept you and give you their next instructions."

"Looks like we've stepped into a war. A cyber war."

"That's exactly what it looks like."

Kitch boarded the *Windy Girl* around 9:00 p.m., one hour before the Strike Force had arranged a call. An audio call only. No video. His eyes popped wide when he saw "Colin" standing before him.

It had to be real for Thornton to pull it off, so he had to be Colin when he was wearing the glasses; that's what he had decided. Anderson introduced them.

"Mr. Buckman, I'd like you to meet Colin MacPherson. Colin, Mr. Buckman."

They formally shook hands.

"Nice to meet you," said Kitch.

Colin just nodded. He went to sit back at the computer console. Anderson took Kitch up on deck. They sat in the cockpit and talked quietly.

"You doing okay?" she asked Kitch.

"Nervous. Understandably. How will this work?" asked Kitch.

"They will call and talk briefly to Thornton, sorry,

Colin. They will already have his profile. They'll probably be doing their search check as we speak."

"Can he pull this off?" asked Kitch.

"For sure. He's a professional, and when he goes undercover, he is that guy. That's why we have to call him Colin. Helps him stay in character. Make things as authentic as possible. We talked all afternoon. He's working on his VPN…"

"His what?"

"Virtual Private Network; it protects his identity when working on the dark web. And he'll be using a TOR browser."

Kitch looked at her with one eyebrow raised.

"There isn't any point in giving you these kinds of details, is there?" said Anderson.

Kitch slowly moved his head left to right.

"Okay, moving right along then. He knows how to get online and do what they need to be done. Better?"

"Much," said Kitch. "Are there 'dirty jobs' on his profile?"

"Absolutely. And he understands how they would have been pulled off. He's up to speed."

"I have no idea what they will ask."

"We talked about those possibilities. If they ask, he'll have some answers. I'm guessing their questions won't be too detailed, or they wouldn't need this guy at all."

"Didn't think of that. Good point."

"So as long as he can dazzle them with lingo, we'll be okay."

"Will he be able to put the next step into action?"

"No. But I will." She smiled. "He'll be wearing an earpiece the whole time, so if he looks at me in a certain way, I give him answers."

"And if they never want to meet, he can do everything remotely. Or you can."

"Exactly. They may send some goons to check him out, but as you just talked last night, we probably have a few days grace before that happens."

"So it will just be the three of us in the room for the call?"

"No, just the two of you. I'll be very much off to the side. Like a piece of furniture."

"Nice furniture."

"Thanks, Kitch. Anything else I should know before we get started?"

"I didn't know anything in the first place."

Anderson laughed. "Okay, let's catch some bad guys."

CHAPTER FIVE

THURSDAY, MAY 28 | MORNING | CANADA

"They bought it, hook, line, and sinker," said Thornton. Colin's glasses were sitting next to the computer, and Thornton had his cap back on.

"Wow, just looking at that ugly shaven mug is all I'd need," said Foster.

"Geek attack for sure; Anderson wasn't exaggerating," said Harrod.

"Does it help you play the role convincingly?" asked Cole.

"Absolutely," said Thornton.

"Then I love it," said Cole. "Let's get to it, things are starting to speed up. Anderson?"

"I'm monitoring that hit team, waiting for them to slip up somewhere so I can gather intel on their next job."

"When you get something, let me know ASAP. Foster and Harrod, you'll start putting together our plan of attack once Anderson gets her info. We want to take this team down this time. We need answers. Thornton, you're putting the next moves for the Strike Force into action?"

Thornton nodded. "Anderson and I are working on that all afternoon."

"Great. Dad, I'm taking you home. Time for you to get some serious sleep. You still haven't recovered from that surgery. We've got this. Thornton, Anderson, I'll come back tonight and you can fill me in on progress. Sound good?"

The team nodded.

"Right. C.H.I.L.," said Cole. They all smiled.

While the Wookies worked on their plan, the Strike Force sent two suits to physically check out the story on Colin MacPherson. They had been sitting outside his apartment for two days, no sign of Colin. His car never moved. They decided to put a tail on Kitch Buckman, who led them right to Colin and the *Windy Girl.*

Anderson poured herself a coffee and one for Colin. He was in role now, preparing. She thought it helped if she thought of him like that.

"Colin." She slid the coffee in front of him. He looked up and nodded, no smile, Colin style.

"Let's set up this hack into the Facebook accounts. The Strike Force wants to expand the campaign using personal phone numbers. Facebook is the best place to get the info, right?"

"Right."

"So, we have to get into these unsecured databases."

"Correct. Phone numbers and emails are gold in cyberattacks. Guess that's what they're leading up to. But what are they attacking?"

"One step at a time. Have a look. Am I moving in the right direction?"

Anderson walked over and looked over Colin's shoulder. "Wow, you're a quick study. Yeah, keep going. Hopefully we can figure out who's leading this campaign before you have to compromise any more information."

"That's the general idea. Okay, I have to concentrate."

Anderson smiled and walked back to her station. She set to work, slowly sipping her coffee, maneuvering her way inside the international cyber web. The thing with covert work on the Internet is that no one can see who you are, but the opposing team's identity and location are hidden as well. She liked that challenge. Her goal was to get a tag on this group that hit Vegas. They were never caught, and there were no clues that the police found. But she did have the clues that Harrod, Foster, and Mac had put together. More reliable than anything.

As she was beginning to spin her own web, a strange message flashed in a corner of her screen. Based on the discussion Thornton had with the Strike Force the night before, she was pretty sure this was them. The message talked about the power after the election, not needing to stay attached, taking an entity down. It was encrypted, but she translated enough to get her fingernails on the edge. National elections were coming up that fall in many countries. She wondered, made notes for Buckman, and then set up a swing back. That's what she liked to call it; it was where she would attach a digital spy to any outgoing messages from this sender and have them come directly into her inbox as well. It had proved invaluable in the past. She was hoping it would yield the same results this time. It was not a quick job. She set to work.

THURSDAY, MAY 28 | AFTERNOON | USA

The Cell arrived separately into Atlantic City. They all had separate rooms on different floors at the Golden Nugget Hotel and Casino. After meeting together at a Denny's for a quick bite, it became clear that this could not be a grab from inside any casino. Their recent successful job at Vegas had euchred them. They wouldn't be able to set foot in a casino. They all had tossed suggestions and ideas on the table. The one involving armoured cars seemed like the best option. They started investigating a viable plan.

THURSDAY, MAY 28 | LATE AFTERNOON | CANADA

Anderson and Thornton were hungry. They had been working all day on chips and beer. They needed some brain food. Anderson said she would head to shore and pick up some microwavable pasta dinners at the local convenience store. It was midweek, late afternoon in May. There weren't many people out and about at that time. She said she wouldn't be long. She climbed on deck and slipped into the dingy. It felt good to get some air.

Over at the dock, the Suits were pulling their second vehicle off the ferry. The had left the first one in the parking lot on the other side of the lake in case something went wrong and they would need to leave without the car. They had been told to continue surveillance on Colin.

The gentle winds collected over the surface of the water, wafting up and catching in Anderson's hair as she made her way to shore in the dingy. She tossed her head like she was playing with the winds. As a girl she had loved running games. She was always the best at hide-and-seek, always found the best places to hide, and no one could catch her as she raced to the home-free tree. Her mother got used to the fact that her daughter would come home with nicks and scrapes, bits of grass and twigs in her hair, mud on her hands and stuck in her shoes, maybe a black eye and a bloody nose, and happy as a little camper.

The motor chugged behind the dingy as she pulled up next to the dock. She was lost in memories as she climbed out and started to tie off when she was grabbed from behind. A black-gloved hand slid over her mouth, and another set of strong arms wrapped around her waist. She was lifted off her feet and carried from the dock toward a waiting vehicle. The initial shock caught Anderson off guard. Within seconds she regained her awareness. Her eyes and instincts did an instantaneous assessment. She swung her fist up toward the face of the man with his gloved hand over her mouth, jamming it against his nose and jarring it upward. His eyes immediately began to water, his nose spurted blood, and his hand dropped away. She then elbowed her other assailant in the ribs and thrust her fist into his chin. As he staggered back, she swung her leg around and up, placing her heel squarely against the side of his head, sending him onto his back. As she turned, the other man lunged at her with a knife, slicing her across her waist, he grabbed her arm and moved to stab her. She danced to one side and the point of the blade entered just under her ribcage. She put her hands together and swung at his head, sending him off balance, and before the other one could get up, she dove into the water, swimming to the *Windy Girl*, blood streaming behind her.

A suit pulled out a gun and fired a shot. She dove. The shot was enough to bring Thornton to the deck. He stood at the bow, looking at where the shots were fired, seeing two men in suits on the dock. They looked back at him. He scanned the docks and water for Anderson. Nothing. He went below and came back with a rifle. He looked right at the men, cocked the rifle, and aimed. The men turned and ran to their vehicle. At that moment he heard his name called at the stern of the boat. He dropped the rifle in the cockpit and ran. Anderson had one hand on the ladder, the other hand reaching up for the next rung. Thornton reached down, grabbed her hand, and pulled her up. She wailed in pain. There was blood everywhere. Thornton ran for bandages, blankets, and the Scotch. He came back and handed her the bottle while he wrapped her wounds in gauze and then wrapped her in the blankets.

"Fuck, I really liked this shirt," she said, trying to find a smile.

"We'll get you another one," said Thornton. "Don't move," he said. "I'm heading for shore. We have to get you to a hospital."

Anderson didn't say anything. She was already in shock and began shivering. She looked up at Thornton, took a swig of Scotch, and closed her eyes, letting the bottle rest beside her.

The Suits got into their vehicle and headed for the ferry, narrowly making it back on the boat. They made a secure call, informing their boss that they had found

Colin. He had a girlfriend and a boat. He was legit. That was their report. No mention of being beaten by a girl and therefore not having her for questioning.

Thornton ran to the cockpit. He had rigged the boat with an immediate and silent release feature in case a quick and stealthy getaway was needed. He decided this was one of those times.

The boat let go of its mooring, and the two silent electric motors, one on each hull, whirred them out of the marina. He increased his speed, deciding not to put up a sail, since they were only crossing the bay. As they were moving toward Queen's Quay harbour, he called Buckman to set up the relay and told him what happened. He then called for a cab and said it was an emergency. Said he'd be at the marina in ten minutes. He sealed and locked the cabin securely as they were crossing, leaving nothing in the cockpit deck. He only carried what would be needed for ID in the hospital. When he entered the marina, he signalled for help, and two guys came running.

"Tie her up. We've had an accident. I need a hospital." With that he ran back and scooped up Anderson, who was now close to unconscious. The guys looked after *Windy Girl*. Thornton ran to the pickup spot as the cab pulled around the corner. He lunged into the back seat with Anderson in his arms.

"St. Michael's Hospital. Hurry."

Back in the stern of the boat, the abandoned bottle of Scotch emptied slowly across the deck.

As Thornton reached the dock at the Marina, Buckman stood behind a cement pillar at the pier due west, waiting for the ferry from the island to arrive. He didn't know how bad Anderson's injuries were, but now he had to zone in. He wanted these Suits. Wanted to know who they were. Wanted to know what they knew. He stayed out of view of those exiting the ferry while maintaining a clear view of those leaving the ship himself. The ferry pulled into its spot, and the gangplank came down. It wasn't high season, but there were always people on the ferry. People began sauntering off, and then he saw them: two men in suits walking briskly. When they got off the gangplank, they broke into a run. Buckman followed. They ran to a parking lot and climbed into a black Audi sedan. Buckman couldn't lose them. He dashed over to a tan Chevy Impala, jimmied the door, and hot-wired the car. He expertly navigated the parking lot in time to see the Audi taking the Gardiner Expressway East.

It helped to have a few other surveillance cars with you at a time like this, but this time it was only Buckman. He swerved in and out of traffic at the exact moments to keep up with the Audi but not be noticed. Not his first rodeo.

The Audi took the Don Valley Parkway northbound.

He wondered if they were heading out of town completely. Buckman stayed a few cars back. The Audi stayed at the speed limit, clearly not wanting to attract attention. Buckman guessed they might be a bit worried about the attention they garnered when Anderson didn't willingly accept their invitation. Of course, they weren't expecting a fiery gal who ate guys like them for breakfast in her homicide days.

Several exits off the highway passed by, and then he saw the Audi move into the right exit lane at York Mills Road West. The guys weren't rushing, so it wasn't a trick to keep them in sight. After a few streets, they turned right and headed north on Leslie Street. Buckman recognized the area. He remembered this cute little brunette he had dated once lived in the suburbs there. He remembered how nice she looked in a tight pair of jeans. He shook his head and pulled himself back into the chase. *If the damn Audi would drive a bit faster, it would make this chase more interesting, and I wouldn't be getting distracted by a fucking memory,* he thought.

They put their turn signal on at Bannatyne Drive and moved into the left turn lane, then veered sharply to the right and started to pick up speed. Buckman veered right, careening on two wheels until gravity pulled all four wheels back on the road. They approached the 401 highway northbound on Leslie at double the speed limit, and the Suits drove through an old wooden fence, half fallen down, into the yard of an abandoned property on the east side of the road.

Buckman kept driving north and pulled into the side of a plaza parking lot, gambling they would keep coming north, which they did, speeding up as they crossed under the 401. They pulled quickly into the North York General Hospital and sat in the parking lot, a cat-and-mouse game.

Buckman was good at the game. He waited across the street. Most would have followed them into the parking lot, but patience had been built into his training. He waited. Patiently. The Suits drove out of the parking lot as if nothing had happened, now satisfied that no one was following them. They slowly made their way back south on Leslie. Buckman maintained a safe distance behind, staying out of their mirrors. Within five minutes, they led him directly to their covert destination. And Buckman knew a safe house is guarded with life itself.

He watched the Audi turn into a driveway of a corner house. There were two other cars there. Buckman kept driving past, slowly, watching in his rear-view mirror as the Suits got out and walked up to the front door. One held his head. *Anderson must have done some damage of her own*, he thought. *Atta girl.* They let themselves in without knocking. Buckman drove around. It was a long street. Good for surveillance. He could move from spot to spot.

He pulled over and parked a few houses up. He sat and waited. Buckman wouldn't consider leaving and coming back in the morning; nope, when he was in, he was in. He started thinking about the stolen car he sat in. How would he explain that to the cops? He wanted to stay off the radar. It was starting to get dark, and he saw a pair of headlights coming up behind him. Closer, bigger, brighter. They pulled up behind him and stopped. *Fuck*, thought Cole. A tall figure got out of the car and started to walk up to Cole's driver's door.

"So, what do we have here?" said a voice. Buckman blinked and cocked his head to one side. Then he turned and leaned out the window.

"You fucking asshole," he said. "What the hell are you doing here?"

"Saving your ass," said Harrod.

"From what?"

"A stolen car report. We figured what you were up to, so we tracked your phone."

"Thanks, man." Buckman got out. "How's Trish?"

"She needed a lot of stitches and lost a lot of blood. They stabbed her pretty good."

"Jesus. Well, let's not make all this for nothing."

"Here are the keys to a Jeep."

"Know where you're taking this?"

"I do. And I'll leave a little thank-you on the front seat."

"Niiice. Foster heading over to Kitch?"

"On his way; can't be too careful right now."

Buckman nodded his agreement. "I'll call you, don't call me." He turned and walked to the Jeep. Harrod got into the Impala and pulled away.

As Buckman climbed into the driver's seat, he saw a change of clothes on the passenger seat: a Leafs ball cap and t-shirt. He laughed and put them on. Harrod would stop at nothing to try and make him a Leafs fan. The other bag had a change of clothes for the next day: black cap and dark blue-collared shirt. Harrod didn't miss a trick. That's why he was a Wookie.

An hour later, the two Suits came out wearing jeans and a sweatshirt. They'd clearly cleaned up. He let them pull out and start down the road before following them to a restaurant down Leslie Avenue. It was a long, square building that looked more like a factory. The building to the south was a factory with loading docks and forklifts still going. Buckman watched the Suits go inside. He waited, timing his entry for when they'd be looking at menus or drinking their beverages. Buckman waited about fifteen minutes before going in, and when he entered the doors, everything slowed down and it all went quiet in his head. He sized the place up instantly; knew where everyone was sitting, what they were wearing, how they were feeling based on body language and mannerisms, who was working. He noticed one of the Suits had a broken nose and the other guy was the one from Kitch's hospital room. They were sending muscles in suits to size up Colin. The pieces were coming together. The Suits were soon drinking beer and eating pizzas.

Buckman went over to a chair adjacent to the table the Suits were sitting in and slumped into the chair, his back to them. It was good that some old habits die hard. He waved to the waitress, who sauntered over. Buckman ordered a Creemore beer on tap with a burger and fries and slipped two twenties into her hands. He knew he'd be leaving before he could settle up. Plus, it was a slow night, so a big tip wouldn't hurt. She was wearing a low-cut Toronto Maple Leafs t-shirt and short shorts; she looked good.

"I like your hat," she said to Buckman.

"I like your team," he said back.

She smiled and walked away. When the Leafs scored, she high-fived Buckman on her way by his table. As they laughed, Buckman noticed the night manager looking sternly their way. She saw him and kept moving, waiting on her tables.

He looked up to the huge television screen and yelled something at one of the Leafs players, just checked into the boards. He put his MI6 pen face down on the tabletop, having first engaged its recording device with a click. It could pick up conversations across a large parking lot. The waitress brought his beer, and he started to drink, pulling his cap a bit lower and intently watching the game while tuning into the conversation behind him. He wasn't worried if he missed some of what they were saying; he'd review it later.

Buckman was glad when his burger was put in front of him. He was hungry. It also gave him something to do while eavesdropping on the goons. He'd been right; they were vetting Colin. Sounded like they thought Anderson was his girlfriend. Hell of a girlfriend. They were saying how they saw Colin come out on the deck of the boat when they fired a shot at the girl. *Perfect,* thought Buckman, *Colin's cover is confirmed.* The Suits got into a bit of an argument over the shot fired. It was sloppy. Could have caused a real problem. Wouldn't have solved a thing to kill the girl. Attracted attention. They were figuring out how they could hide that from their boss. Comedy hour.

Buckman was halfway through his burger and fries and halfway through his pint. He had to stop and cheer when the Leafs scored. He was wearing the cap and shirt. The Suits were almost through their pizzas. They talked about a meeting the next day in Yorkville, at a candle shop. Buckman drained his beer. He had to leave before they did. He kept his back to them as he left the restaurant, grabbing a few final fries from his plate on the way, and went out to his Jeep parked down the road. He sat, watching and waiting. He saw the waitress come out for a quick smoke, obviously on her break. The manager approached her. Buckman heard him yell but couldn't quite make out his words. He grabbed her and threw her up against the wall. She struggled, and he was clearly going to slap her, but Buckman moved across the street and was there to grab his wrist. He started twisting it, tossed him against the wall, and as he bounced back, Buckman's fist was there to greet his face. Buckman grabbed him before he fell and put him in a chokehold, turning on the pressure.

"Lay a hand on a Leafs fan again and I'll come back to finish the job," said Buckman. He dropped the guy to the ground, touched the brim of his hat to the waitress, and went back to his Jeep. He thought he had missed the Suits, but then he saw their car pulling out. By the time Cole caught up with them, he saw them pull into the same safe house driveway and walk inside.

He pulled up behind another vehicle parked on the road a few houses down and settled in for the night. He set up his motion-sensor video recorder, an MI6 trinket he always had good use for, and pointed it at the safe house. If something started happening, it would sound an alert, waking up Buckman. That way he could get a bit of shuteye. Before reclining his seat, he listened to the recording from the restaurant. Near the end, the meeting time at the candle shop was confirmed: 11:00 a.m. He sent the whole audio file to Anderson. She would deal with it when she got back.

He reclined his seat and closed his eyes.

THURSDAY, MAY 28 | LATE AFTERNOON | BRITAIN

The Data Protection Commission was in a tizzy. They didn't know how to contain the leak of personal information of millions of people. The supervisor had been brought in. He dialled the number of the director at Facebook's European headquarters in Dublin, Ireland.

"Siobhan?'

"Here."

"What the fuck is going on?"

"We're looking into it?"

"That's it? That's all you have to say?"

"What do you want me to say, Phil?"

"This is quickly becoming a matter of national security. This isn't just Europe; we've discovered it is happening in North America as well. Millions and millions of citizen's personal data has been hacked."

"Yes, we are aware."

"You're aware. Excellent. You're aware then that we are now experiencing targeted attacks."

"What do you mean attacks?"

"Some people in my office are getting texts and emails sending them information that will lead to unrest and attacks on the leaders of each government. We have to shut this down. Stop the leaks."

"It's not like turning off a tap, Phil. It's coming from

databases that are untraceable."

"I thought Facebook was next to God. You're telling me you're not able to do a thing?"

"We're working on it."

"Fuck, Siobhan, that's bullshit and you know it. If we can bury you guys, we will. I'll deal with this on my end then."

Phil turned to his team.

"Okay, every email, every text anyone in this office receives or if a friend of family receives one, I want to know. Let's start digging out of this mess before we're buried. Who the fuck is doing this?!"

THURSDAY, MAY 28 | LATE AFTERNOON | ITALY

While the Data Protection Commission dealt with a massive hack of personal information in Britain, the Palazzo Montecito Rio in Italy was being stormed by citizens calling for the resignation of the leader. The national gendarmerie had to be called in so riots would not escalate.

FRIDAY, MAY 29 | MORNING | CANADA

Standard operating hospital procedure meant Anderson had to be taken out of the hospital in a wheelchair. She was not impressed. She also wasn't impressed that she had been made to stay overnight. It was only twenty-odd stitches, which didn't seem earth-shattering to her. But apparently it was the blood loss. It had been significant. Swimming vigorously with a hole in your body is apparently not a good practice for life extension. Said she'd been lucky the stab wound under her ribs hadn't punctured her lung. They put a few stitches there as well. And a few butterfly bandages, because Trish had asked nicely. The doctor cleared her early that morning, and Thornton wheeled her away. Once out on the sidewalk, she stood up and took Thornton's arm. They didn't say anything or look at each other. Thornton hailed a cab, helped Trish inside, and gave the address of the marina where *Windy Girl* awaited.

"I'm okay, Bill," Trish said.

"Don't scare me like that again," he said.

"I'll try not to," she said and turned her head to look at him, smiling.

His head turned at the same time, and their eyes met, softened. Without blinking, he noticed the flecks of grey in her steely blue irises, and she looked deeply into his warm brown orbs. For that moment, there was nothing else. No cab. No cars passing by. No honking. No sirens. No Wookies. No injuries. It was like they had interlaced lenses as one would interlace fingers, and the touch was warm and electric all at the same time. They were drawn toward each other, closer, closer…

"Shall I take a different route?" hollered the cab driver. "There seems to be an accident up ahead."

Thornton readjusted in his seat. Anderson leaned over and looked out the window.

"Sure, sure," said Thornton. "Take the other route. We need to get there quickly."

Bill looked over at Trish as she gazed out the window, yearning to have the moment back again.

"Here you go," said the cab driver. Thornton passed some bills over the front seat and climbed out of the cab. Anderson was already walking toward the boat. He followed behind.

The boys had done a good job tying it up. Thornton and Anderson hopped on board. He unlocked the hatch, and Anderson went directly below to her computers. She had to make sure everything was secure. She was also starving. She poked her head back up as Thornton was readying the boat for sailing.

"Hey, before we cast off, any way you could run over to that snack bar and grab me a dog and a coffee, or muffin, or all the above? I'm starving."

"And your last helot died of what?"

"Very funny. Would you mind?"

"Course not. I'm pretty hungry too. The stuff that comes out of a hospital vending machine is worse than eating plastic. I'll be right back."

Trish watched him go. Watched the way his shoulders swayed. Watched the way he firmly planted his feet with every step. Watched his hips. She moistened her lips, drew in a deep breath, and went to her computers. She was glad to get back to work.

There were messages popping up everywhere. She organized them into files and started perusing the lists, looking for any hint or clue, any taste of next steps. She was deeply absorbed when Thornton jumped down and put a bag with a hamburger, hotdog, fries, muffin, an apple, a banana, and two coffees in front of her.

"That should hold you for a while. I'm going to cast off. We'll sail over to the marina east of the city."

"The spit?"

"Exactly."

"Thornton, take a look at this."

"What am I looking at?" he asked, sipping his own coffee as Anderson took larger mouthfuls of the burger and a few fries at the same time.

"Here," she mumbled with her mouthful. "This

encrypted message is basically someone talking in Europe, and then they mention the Absecon Lighthouse."

"Isn't that in Atlantic City?"

"It is."

"And they have casinos there."

"They do."

"And you're thinking…"

"The next hit is going to be in Atlantic City."

"Nice work. Not bad for someone who's just sucked back a few litres of blood." She looked up at him and stopped chewing. "Sorry, not the best subject when you're eating, I guess." She nodded and started chewing again. "Food hit the spot?"

"Oh yeah!" she said, popping more fries into her mouth and washing them down with gulps of coffee.

"Time to get the *Windy Girl* into action."

"Can you contact the Wookies while I grab more info here?" she asked.

"Absolutely," he said. "Wookies need to get into action."

"You can do that and sail?"

"It's amazing what us helots are capable of." He winked and headed to the cockpit.

While Anderson and Thornton were relocating the *Windy Girl* and processing their information, Buckman decided to drive over to Yorkville. He had been woken a few times by his video alert, but it wasn't the Suits. It was about 9:30 a.m. and still no movement. Clearly their encounter with Anderson was more than they had expected. He wanted to get to the meeting spot well before the Suits to get a good parking spot out front and survey the candle shop for a while. It was at least a thirty-minute drive over. Plus, he was desperate for a coffee. He knew where the safe house was if no one showed up at 11:00 a.m.

He began navigating the streets of Toronto, lingering morning rush hour traffic still a bit of an issue. It was good he had left when he did. He stopped at Tim Hortons drive-thru on the way over, grabbing a breakfast burrito and a large black coffee. He placed the burrito on the seat beside him and clutched the coffee in his hand. He took a long, luxurious sip. The dark, steaming liquid brought an energy and warmth into his veins. He took a deep breath. It was a sunny day, and he was stiff from sitting in the Jeep all night. He decided to find a bench with a good vantage point and eat there.

He pulled into Cumberland Drive, which was relatively quiet at that time in the morning, making it easy to find a parking spot on the street. He drove along looking for the candle shop. It was one of the shops underneath, steps down from the sidewalk to the entrance. *Wick-ed* was printed in large letters on the banner above the door, and candles of all shapes and sizes posed behind the display window. That was how Yorkville was set up; a shop or restaurant up top, another below. Benches and trees, small grass areas. It was a trendy part of Toronto, and soon it would be filled with people. Buckman circled around and came back up Cumberland, finding the perfect spot, a few car lengths before the entrance to *Wick-ed*. He popped on the other black ball cap and changed into a plain blue long-sleeve collared shirt, then slid on his FTO144 sunglasses. He grabbed his burrito and coffee, stepped out of the Jeep, and settled onto a bench warmed by the early morning spring sun, just down and across from the candle shop. He waited. It was 10:30.

At 10:45, a young woman wearing stylishly ripped jeans, a multicoloured batik blouse, and a wave of pink in her hair walked toward the candle shop on the opposite side of the street. She wore sunglasses and carried a large box. She went down the steps, put the box down, and juggled a tangle of keys before finding the one to open the door. Buckman figured she was the shop-girl for the day. She fit right into the Yorkville vibe. He kept sipping his coffee, watching the store window. Switches must have been flicked on because lights filled the previously dark space and candles came to life in the window. They didn't just sell tapers. These were works of art where light illuminated shapes from within. Even from where he sat, it was entrancing.

As he took this all in, his trained eye caught the image of the two Suits in the driver's-side mirror on the sports car to his left. He adjusted his hat and brought the burrito to his mouth as they passed in front of him. He watched them without turning his head. They were five minutes early. They crossed the street and walked down the steps into *Wick-ed*. Buckman sipped his coffee, waiting. He finished his burrito and compressed the wrapper, tucking it into his jeans pocket.

Other shopkeepers started arriving, opening their stores. More people collected in the area, carrying coffees or ice cream cones, all enjoying the spring weather. A woman started walking toward the candle shop on the opposite side of the street. She stood out. There was no pause in her step to enjoy the sun or the morning. No coffee. No window-shopping. Her stiletto heels clicked irritably on the sidewalk. Her Gucci handbag was looped over her forearm. She wore a black A-line skirt to the top of her knee, cream blouse, and waist-flared black jacket. Her hair was pulled back into a bun. Buckman peered more closely. He recognized her. His eyes followed her as she made her way down the steps into *Wick-ed*. He remembered. She was the security advisor to the Canadian PM. Seconds after she walked down the steps, two very large Suits, clearly her security detail, followed her and stood outside the entrance to the candle shop.

Buckman sucked back the last drops of his coffee, wishing he had chosen an extra large. He waited. His phone vibrated in his pocket. He pulled it out and saw a text from Thornton:

Moored off the Leslie Street Spit Marina now.
Falcon good, back to work.
Next activity Atlantic City.
Pull in Wookies. Prepare.

Then a text from Foster:

Package Secure.

Things were moving. Buckman kept tipping up his empty coffee cup. The sidewalks were speeding up with people. He slowed everything down, taking out the sound, and zoomed in on the shop as people entered and exited. Time played in the sun shadows on the sidewalk. At 1:00 p.m., the two large Suits moved to one side, and the security advisor walked up the steps, closely followed by the other two Suits from the safe house. Buckman stood, blending with the pedestrians. He kept his eye on the targets as he moved toward his Jeep. All five climbed into a black Suburban up the street. Buckman slid into the Jeep's driver's seat and pulled out, leaving two cars between him and the targets. The vehicle navigated the downtown core, battling its way onto the Allen Expressway North and finally the 401 West. Buckman stayed a safe distance back. They took the exit leading to Pearson International Airport. Buckman was right on their tail.

FRIDAY, MAY 29 | EVENING | CANADA

Thornton and Anderson brought Harrod and Foster up to speed below deck on *Windy Girl*. They liked the new marina they were moored off, more out of the way. Foster felt they should've been there in the first place. While they were debating the merits of mooring options, a message came in from Cole.

"He's off to France," said Anderson. "Gone Suit fishing apparently. So, we're looking after Atlantic City on our own, boys."

"That means you have to be Thornton for a few days," said Harrod. "Colin will go on a vacation."

"And you'll need hair and a beard," said Foster. "No telling who is hanging around right now. Let's keep your cover safe."

"Well, speaking of cover, before we go anywhere, I have to initiate another piece of the agenda. They want the hacking to intensify. The whispering to get nasty."

"Nasty?" asked Foster.

"Not that kind of nasty, Foster," said Thornton. Foster rolled his eyes.

"So, I've figured out how to do just enough so they see the job is being carried out, but I've built in an escape route," said Anderson.

"The source of the hack is untraceable," said

Thornton. "All initiatives and commands will disappear, completely, not even a smudge left in the cloud, in forty-eight hours."

"Excellent," said Harrod.

"How long will all that take?" asked Foster.

"As long as it will take to push this little button here," said Anderson.

"She's been working on this all afternoon," said Thornton.

"Our rock star," said Harrod. "So, push the button."

"Done," said Anderson.

"Re: Atlantic City and the hit team, whatta we know, Anderson?" asked Thornton.

"Okay, well, the chatter I'm picking up suggests they plan to do something on Monday, after a weekend of money exchanging hands in casinos. They're staying at the Golden Nugget Casino. They have four rooms booked. The rest is too sketchy to put money on. We need to get in there fast and do some intel."

"Right. So, we leave tonight," said Harrod.

"Agreed," said Anderson. "Our flight is already booked. We're staying at Caesars."

"The place by the beach?" asked Foster.

"Really? Hoping for some bikini tanning time?" asked Thornton.

"Hey, a girl's gotta dream," said Anderson. "Of course."

"Fair enough."

Anderson handed out papers to each of them and a brown baggie. "Here's the name you're travelling under. Your room is booked in that name as well. And earpieces, burner phones." She passed them around.

"First course of action?" asked Foster.

"Get a bug into the room or rooms of these mercenaries. We've gotta figure out what's going on, fast."

"Right. Each of us will watch one of the rooms, and when they leave, get in, get out. If we get all rooms, great. One, so be it. We'll connect midmorning for an update," said Thornton.

"Look for phones left to charge, laptops, clothing, anything personal they would keep close to them most of the time," said Anderson.

"Anything else?" asked Thornton.

"Let's do it," said Harrod.

CHAPTER SIX

FRIDAY, MAY 29 | EVENING | CANADA

"Have you seen how many calls have come in during the last hour?" asked an employee at the Parliament buildings in Ottawa.

"It's insane. People are asking if these messages about the PM are true."

"But a lot are becoming hate messages. They are believing these whispers."

"Sure, they're going right to their personal text messages."

"My family called me. They are all getting them now. Asking me how their phone number was exposed. Asking me if this stuff is true. Was our PM involved in that drug cartel? It's crazy."

"Did anyone contact the Canadian Security Intelligence Service?"

"CSIS? They're just as confused as we are."

"What are they saying?"

"Facebook's database of personal info has been hacked."

"Holy fuck. So it's not just our country."

"Hell, no. We're getting reports from Italy, France, Britain, the US. Who knows how far-reaching this goes?"

"In the newest batch of emails and FB posts, the messages are getting more specific. Smears and compromising connections to the leaders."

"Any truth to them?"

"There's always some truth, but it's a very slanted twisting of the truth. Problem is, people are starting to buy it."

"Elections are coming up."

"Exactly."

"Are we looking at election-fixing here?"

"If it is, it's on a scale no one has seen before."

"But the current leaders are being trashed, so who is the other option? Who is this saviour they keep referring to?"

"That, my friend, is the billion-dollar question."

SATURDAY, MAY 30 | EARLY MORNING | FRANCE

Buckman awoke in his window seat near the back of the plane. He had one of the last seats on the Airbus A350. He tried to move his pretzeled body out of the cramped seat. Travelling coach never seemed to get better. More than 250 people in the rows ahead of Buckman were feeling the same effects of the squashed seating. The Suits and security advisor he'd followed from *Wick-ed* were comfortably in first class. They'd probably be sipping mimosas by now.

Announcements were being made to put all chair backs into the upright position for landing. He wondered why they still said that, because they certainly didn't recline enough to make a difference. He saw the fading evening lights of Paris approaching out of his window, the Eiffel Tower blinking like a French tease, the beginning glow of the advancing sunrise. It was 4:00 a.m. in Paris. It would be approximately 5:00 a.m. once they cleared customs. He felt the landing gear jolt beneath him. He snugged up his seatbelt as the Airbus neared the runway. For such an early flight, they must have to be somewhere in a hurry. Once through customs, he would have to keep a keen eye. He couldn't afford to lose them now.

The aircraft touched down, and some people clapped. Buckman often wondered why they clapped; glad the pilot hadn't fallen asleep, happy to soon be out of the cramped seats, grateful the plane didn't do a belly flop? All good reasons to clap. Still, pilots were just doing their jobs. Buckman prepared to do his own job once they connected with the gate tunnel. As they cruised toward the terminal, the plane started to slow down. Buckman looked out his window, but they were still a long way from the any building. In fact, they were just on the edge of the tarmac, near the edge of the airport proper. And the Airbus came to a complete stop.

Instantly, he knew what was happening. Passengers were told to remain in their seats. A staircase was wheeled over to the airplane, and he watched as the Suits and the security advisor exited the plane and climbed into a black SUV. He noted the license plate. *Fuck*, he thought. There was only one person he could call that could track that vehicle now. He made the call. There was no time to lose.

SATURDAY, MAY 30 | MORNING | ITALY

It had all looked so good at the beginning. The Strike Force had created such a simple, smooth plan. And then he had been offered a lot of money by a Chinese businessman. He had said no. Then he was told to stop, surrender the agenda, or his sister would live out her days in a Chinese prison. He still had no idea how the Chinese contact had got wind of the Strike Force's plan. But he did know why they contacted him: his huge debts, and when that didn't work, his sister sitting right at their fingertips.

It wasn't a huge leap to understand how Ian found out that he was making other deals. Betraying the Strike Force. That was his job. Hacking computer systems. Manipulating information. But Ian didn't know the full situation. Of course, Ian assumed correctly he was going to sell them all out, but the situation his sister was in left him no choice. Rather than tell the rest of the Strike Force, he was going to the British PM. And that would mean China wouldn't get what they wanted, and his sister would be their slave for life. Maybe that was why Ian had gone to the PM, to make sure someone knew what was going on if all the Strike Force was taken out and their agenda moved into Chinese hands.

Either way, Ian had to be taken out. And the Strike Force couldn't know it was him. He wouldn't slowly leak information to the Chinese, since they were demanding, and then they would take over when they saw fit.

He poured himself another drink and lit another cigarette. He had to keep his cool. Had to play it cool. His sister's life depended on it. The next meeting was at the safe house in France in three hours. He had a plane to catch.

SATURDAY, MAY 30 | LATE MORNING | FRANCE

As Buckman finished his call, the airbus resumed its taxi to the terminal gate. Mac had contacts everywhere and favours to cash in on. This would be one of those favours. She called an Interpol intelligence colleague at the Airport Special Intelligence Division and gave him a watered down version of the situation. Less authorities knew the better. Mac was rarely questioned on decisions she made. Meanwhile, the SUV carrying the security advisor waited on the tarmac while a Lufthansa flight crossed in front of them on their way to their gate. The delay gave valuable seconds to the team Mac had managed to put together. They were used to scrambling. Mac had given them the license plate and vehicle description, and within minutes the team tailed the SUV on the highway. Then she had arranged for a Peugeot 907 to be waiting outside the terminal for Buckman once he had raced through the airport after clearing customs. She figured the Peugeot would give him the kickstart he needed to catch up with his Suits.

Time seemed to move like molasses for Buckman until his ass hit the driver's seat of the dark blue Peugeot. He was sent the current location of the SUV and he raced to catch up, glad everyone in Europe drove like madmen. He would fit right in. Once he caught up, no one would be the wiser. But Mac knew. And she was always good to have in your back pocket. He owed her. And she knew it. He couldn't wait for her to collect.

SATURDAY, MAY 30 | AFTERNOON | USA

Thornton, a.k.a. Doc, went directly to the Golden Nugget Hotel upon landing in Atlantic City and installed small surveillance cameras on each floor where one of the Cell had booked a room. They had rooms on four different floors. Anderson had done her homework. Early the next morning, before anyone had woken up, each Wookie would camouflage in a housekeeping utility room on each floor of a Cell member's room. From there, they would watch the hallway on their phones, images sent via the cameras Doc had installed. When the target left the room, they would know. At 10:45 a.m., Harrod, a.k.a. 2Tall, signalled that a large man had left the room, cap and glasses obscuring his face. When he entered the elevator and the doors closed, 2Tall was in his room. Minutes later, Foster, a.k.a. Tuna, said a small Asian woman had left. He was in and out of her room in minutes. There was no action from the other two rooms. By 11:30 a.m., the Wookies had left the hotel and were meeting at Caesars.

"We're meeting on the beach?" asked Tuna. "Seriously?"

"Of course. A little sand. A little sun. This may be my only opportunity. I figure they went for brunch, so we have some time," said Falcon.

"We could all use a little relaxation time," said 2Tall.

"And Falcon is still sporting a lot of stitches," said Doc.

"You doing okay?" asked Tuna.

"Painkillers are a wonderful thing," she said. Then, responding to Tuna's look of concern, "I'm okay. I will be. It's well wrapped, you know, in case things get physical."

"Well, let's hope it doesn't have to come to that."

"Yeah, let's hope," said 2Tall. "Meantime, let's make sure our guns are clean and loaded. And that we have a good lot of extra mags with us."

"Fair point," said Tuna. "Anyone hungry? I see a nice little burger bar over there."

"Excellent," said 2Tall, "I'm starving." They got up and started walking over to the food stand. They had all agreed it was safer to use their handles during the whole time spent in Atlantic City.

"Hang on," said Tuna. "I'm getting something on the device I planted in her room. We struck gold, my friends. They all gathered in that one room. The device is picking up the conversation."

"Can we listen and eat?" asked 2Tall.

"Shhhhh," they all said in unison.

"Guess not," said 2Tall to himself.

"Bit unclear, but I don't think they're going to hit a casino, too much security after Vegas. But they did mention the Trump Plaza Hotel."

"So, they either heard about Vegas…"

"Or they did Vegas."

"My money is on the second one."

"They're going to hit armoured vehicles, taking away the cash load after the weekend," said Tuna.

"So, Monday."

"Sounds that way. They must have thrown a piece of clothing on the table where I put the bug. It's all static now."

"Good start. Falcon, see what you can find out about armoured cash delivery vehicles in this town. I'm going to check out the Trump Plaza."

"We'll keep listening in, see if they come back and share more secrets," said Tuna.

"After we get a burger and a beer," said 2Tall. Tuna pursed his lips and nodded in agreement.

Doc and Falcon laughed. "Okay. Let's meet up around 7:00 p.m. at the bar at Caesars."

Tuna and 2Tall headed toward the bar in the Golden Nugget. They were deep in conversation and when they passed through the doors, 2Tall almost walked smack into another person. He turned his head and looked directly into the face of Sarah Thompson. They both remained expressionless.

"Well, I'll be," said 2Tall. "Of all the gin joints in all the world…"

"Actually, it's 'of all the gin joints in all the towns in

all the world…'"

"Thanks for the correction. Some things never change. Sarah, my buddy Foster."

"Pleasure." She reached her right hand forward.

"And mine," said Tuna as their hands connected. "You guys clearly know each other."

"Back in military days," said Sarah. "You here on business?"

"Strictly pleasure," said 2Tall.

"You do that?" she said.

"Here and there. How about you."

"Vacay," she answered. "Don't say it."

2Tall smiled. "Wasn't gonna. Well, I don't want to keep you from your fun. Maybe we can have a drink while you're in town."

"Maybe," she said. She turned and walked out of the building.

Tuna and 2Tall went and sat at the bar. They ordered two pints and burgers with fries. Loaded.

"Fuck me," said 2Tall.

"What are the fucking odds?" said Tuna.

"Well, pretty high, I guess. I mean, we are tracking them."

"Think she knew?"

"I don't know. Hard to tell. So hard to read her. That was always the problem."

"Think it will change their plans?"

"Well, we'll have to keep listening. But I doubt it. Too much would have gone into this job. Think it will change ours?" The two pints were placed in front of them.

"Well, that's better," said Tuna after downing a large part of his pint.

"Absolutely," agreed 2Tall, wiping the foam from his mouth.

"Change our plans?" said Tuna. "Well, our plans are based on their plans."

"But my cover has been blown."

"She doesn't know you're here as 2Tall."

"True. If they pick up any chatter, it will be our handles."

"Plus, it won't really matter if you're Harrod or 2Tall once on the job…you'll have a gun in your hand." 2Tall laughed.

"More than one, I'm hoping," said 2Tall. "Think she bought the holiday thing?"

"Not even a little bit."

"Didn't think so," said 2Tall.

"Then again, she really has no clue why you are here. Maybe you've picked up a gambling problem."

"Maybe I have," said 2Tall.

"Well, that's your story…"

"And I'm sticking to it." They picked up their mugs,

clinked, and bottomed up.

"Well, they will carry out their plan or they won't. Simple," said Tuna. "Either way, we'll be ready."

SATURDAY, MAY 30 | LATE AFTERNOON | FRANCE

After driving for almost an hour, Buckman pulled up behind the car Mac had described. It was idling on the side of the road, apparently waiting for him. He got out and walked up to the driver's door. They conversed in French, in which Buckman was fluent. The driver said the SUV he had been ordered to follow had pulled into a farm lane up ahead. He didn't want to go in without further instructions. Buckman thanked him and reminded him he would be happy to return the favour whenever the need arose. The driver said he would wait on the road, just in case backup was needed. Buckman nodded his thanks. He left his car where it was and headed in on foot.

Buckman nudged up to the farm's entrance. He remembered a similar location on a mission with one of his mentors from the British SAS. That was when he had learned the art of photographing a location with his mind, locking every detail into place for future use. His life might depend on it. He thought this could be one of those moments.

He took in the lay of the land: long driveway, small brick house on one side of the winding lane, barn on the other. Fenced paddock where some cows stood chewing their cud. There were cars parked haphazardly near the barn. There were armed men standing outside every entrance to the small house. Buckman counted three, and one guard near the vehicles. The location was similar to what his dad had described in Italy. The Strike Force obviously had many meeting locations. All the guards were carrying FAMAS bullpup assault rifles. *Those fucking things are no joke*, thought Buckman. They had a firing rate of 1,100 rounds of 5.56 per minutes. *I wouldn't stand a chance trying to dodge those suckers,* he thought. *Not to mention the H&Ks strapped to their hips. These guys have more capacity magazines than the entire French army. Jesus.*

He inched his way up the last part of the lane, staying close to the thickets lining the narrow roadway. The elements were with him. The wind had picked up but was blowing at right angles to the house, taking the sound and smell of Buckman away from the guards. He made his way stealthily and with the help of the next gust of wind dashed into a thicket at the top of the lane, off the edge of the lawn near the house. He crouched down and waited.

A tiny twig snapped under his foot, and the guard's head whipped around. Buckman saw he had quickly shifted his weapon into the ready position and had begun walking toward the trees where the sound had originated. Cole sat like a hare that could smell the breath of its predator. He waited until the guard was within range and then nimbly shot a toxic dart from his watch. It hit the guard in the neck, and he fell like a sequoia. Buckman crawled out from under the branches, grabbed him by the collar, and dragged him under the tree, tucking him behind the trunk, out of view. He pulled the radio off the guard's belt, slung his weapon over his shoulder, shoved the handgun into the back of his pants, and headed over to cover his post. The windows were covered with a light kind of curtain fabric, allowing him to see shapes in the room. He peered closely and could make out a large round table with five figures sitting around it.

He pulled out his MI6 recorder pen. It had been paying for itself over the last few days. Too bad they would have to part ways. MI6 wouldn't be handing him another one in the near future. He could activate it to immediately send its recording to a computer device, phone, or tablet. He selected his phone and Anderson's phone. He clicked it on and placed it on the window ledge. Then he moved away from the window. His radio beeped.

"*Ça va?*" asked the voice.

"*Oui, ça va bien,*" answered Buckman.

"*J'ai entendu un bruit,*" the voice said.

"*Je n'ai rien entendu,*" replied Buckman.

"*J'arrive,*" said the voice.

Buckman didn't want anyone else to deal with, and he certainly didn't want any weapons fired. He wasn't as big as the other guard and would be spotted immediately.

Weapons would be fired. He moved himself off his mark and around the side of the house. He heard the guard approaching, quietly calling the name of the other guard. Buckman waited, and the minute his head appeared around the corner of the house, he shot his last dart into the man's cheek. It wasn't as effective as in the neck. The guy's eyes widened, and he reached for his weapon. Cole shoved it out of the guy's hands, willing the poison to take effect. Before anything else could happen, Buckman wheeled around and launched the heel of his boot square into the side of the guy's head. That, and the poison beginning to seep into his veins, dropped him hard. Buckman didn't waste a moment. He dragged him around the side of the house, out of view, and slithered back down the lane in the camouflage of the trees. He ran for his car, waving to the waiting vehicle, dove into the driver's seat, and they sped off down the road.

SATURDAY, MAY 30 | EVENING | USA

"Are you fucking kidding me?" asked Berea.

"No, I'm not," said Cobra.

"Your fucking military trainer? OMG," said Berea.

"Do we pull out?" asked Dagger.

"We can't, no time left," said Cobra. "We have to finish this job, then we're done with them."

"Do they have anything on us?" asked Berea.

"Of course," said Dagger. "They always do."

"Do you think he knows anything?" asked DangPa.

"Hard to tell, he's hard to read," said Cobra.

"Well, I say we proceed as planned," said Dagger. "There's no way they can figure out what we're organizing in a day."

"Any bugs in the room?" asked Berea.

"I combed the whole room when I came in," said DangPa. "I always do. Nothing."

"Okay, so how's it gonna go down on Monday?" asked Berea. "Let's put it in place and then hide tomorrow, stay low."

"Right. Here's the plan," said Cobra.

"Sarah Thompson?" said Falcon.

"The girl without the finger who lost the button?" said Doc.

"Who probably shot Ian?" said Tuna.

"Her?" said Falcon.

"Yup," said 2Tall.

"Are we compromised?"

"I don't think so," said 2Tall.

"I know so," said Tuna.

"How?"

"They didn't find my bug, and I got a lot of details."

"Okay, whatta we know? Tuna, you go first."

"It appears that they are going to hit two armoured vans Monday morning. Because of the world high-stakes games this weekend, they figure the vans will be transporting well over five mil."

"Where?"

"Behind the Trump Plaza."

"Why there? And why do you keep saying vans?' asked Doc.

"I can answer that," said Falcon. "I learned that the Armored Car Company in Atlantic City is moving away from the big, heavy, marked trucks to smaller unmarked vans, mostly black or grey."

"Less conspicuous," said 2Tall.

"Exactly. Unless…"

"You're a mercenary," said 2Tall.

"What else?" asked Doc.

"Well, you asked why behind the Trump Plaza," said Falcon. "That was interesting. I had to pull in a few favours because this was more of a need-to-know piece of info than something I could scavenge online. Turns out the drivers of the money vans get a little hungry before finishing their drop. They've got into the habit of parking behind the Plaza, and a friend of theirs who cooks there comes out with breakfast for two plus."

"Plus what?"

"Plus the guards in each van. About six people. Totally against all rules, but since they downsized from the big trucks and took the markings off, things settled down, no one really paid attention, and it became a nice little habit."

"But the hit team found out as well," said Tuna.

"Exactly. These guys put in a lot of overtime, so I guess they figured they deserved this little break. Thing is, they turn off their GPS for that half hour so the dispatcher doesn't know their location."

"What is that location?" asked 2Tall.

"A vacant parking lot used for overflow on busy nights but pretty deserted in the morning hours. Pacific and Mississippi Avenues," said Tuna.

"Nice little plan," said Falcon.

"Maybe not so much on Monday morning," said Doc.

"Okay, so tomorrow we need to check out a few things and make sure all the weapons are ready to go. 2Tall and Tuna, you look after the weapons and vehicles. Falcon, you and I will go over and do a recon of the site at this parking lot. We'll all meet back here at 7:00 p.m. tomorrow night and finalize our plan for Monday."

"Sounds like you may even have time for a little more sand between your toes, Falcon," said Tuna.

"I can only hope," said Falcon.

SUNDAY, MAY 31 | FRANCE

Buckman sat in his hotel room in Paris playing the recording over and over from his phone. He wanted to make sure he hadn't missed any detail. His notes needed to be meticulous. He couldn't distinguish all the five different voices in the barn. Two were very clear, the others were audible but would not be identified without voice recognition software. A lot of tension was in that room, that much was apparent. He picked that up through the covered window. They were pleased with the job Colin was doing. That was good. There were heated words from one man. Buckman couldn't make out what it was about. Too garbled. The accents didn't help. They talked about a next phase to be executed in an open and exposed setting they had planned over a year ago: a pro-am golf tournament to be held at the Albatros course at Le Golf National, in Guyancourt, France, where the legendary Ryder Cup was scheduled to happen in three years. World leaders from the G8 and their security advisors would be in France for their annual meeting fast approaching. They had all been invited to the golf tournament. All had accepted. Buckman listened as details of the tournament were discussed, matching leaders and advisors with golf celebrities, caddies, the gala dinner. Leaders were vain. They loved celebrity events. They began discussing a united collective, but the loud voices of the guards began. They had discovered Buckman's handiwork. More yelling, and then the pen was discovered. There was a loud crack of sound in the recording. Buckman pursed his lips, knowing the pen had done its duty. He wished he had learned more about this united collective, but he definitely had more information than when he arrived.

Buckman was starting to put the pieces of the puzzle together. And after putting the voices through voice recognition, he would be even closer. The golf tournament was key. He had to get on the list of pros. He had to play. That was where the final pieces would all come together. The Wookies needed to get to France. He hoped Anderson could do the voice rec ASAP, discover the date of this golf tournament, and get him on the list. But he knew they were knee-deep in their own mission, and what happened there could be the keystone.

Everything was hovering like a hawk circling its prey, calculating the precise moment to dive.

MONDAY, JUNE 1 | MORNING | USA

Showtime, 8:30 a.m. The two armoured money vans pulled into the empty parking lot behind Trump Plaza, as they had been doing every day. They pulled up and parked at right angles to each other so the drivers could sit together and yet still keep an eye on the vans. They started to get out just as the cook came from the kitchen with their morning feast. The driver said thanks, and they sat down at the picnic table to enjoy the best coffee in town with crunchy bacon and warm, fluffy pancakes. They were lost in taste sensations.

The Wookies were in their hiding places they had scoped out on Sunday; 2Tall and Tuna were in the garage around a corner close by. Falcon walked toward the parking lot from the nearby beach, wearing tourist sunglasses and big-brimmed sunhat, a colourful pink and yellow sarong tied around her waist, a pale yellow crop top, and a big green woven beach bag over her shoulder filled with handy weapons and a diet Cola. Doc hid behind a dumpster, his eyes on the whole area. The Wookies would await his command. They were all armed with their Glock handguns, recently cleaned by Tuna and 2Tall, extra mags on their persons.

Suddenly, smoke came out from below each van; it looked like tossed smoke grenades. Had to be from the

Cell. It was just enough to startle the guards, who scrambled off the picnic table and headed for the doors of the vans. Then, like lightning, the four members of the Cell appeared. Cobra opened fire with her favourite weapon, hitting several of the guards. The other three also opened fire and then moved in fast. Only two of the guards were able to return fire, having been caught with their pants down and forks up.

The Wookies moved fast in reply, guns drawn. Doc opened fire on the Cell, going through his first clip in a microsecond and then reloading in record time. 2Tall fired and hit DangPa in the leg. She returned fire. Berea had 2Tall's forehead in his sights when Doc fired two shots, double-tapped both to the centre of Berea's forehead. He was dead before he hit the ground. The Cell team didn't know what was happening. They had no idea who was shooting at them. The guards were out of the fight, dead, wounded, or just scared, but they were all on the ground. Dagger quickly saw that things had gone sideways. Cobra yelled at him to fire back. She was trying to reload her long gun while firing with a handgun, all the while trying to grab DangPa, who was hit but still moving. Dagger hollered to Cobra to get the hell out of there and started running down the alley. Doc and Falcon were right on his tail. Tuna, forgetting his age and that he was supposed to be retired, jumped for the wounded DangPa. He held her down, but she fought hard. Cobra opened fire again. 2Tall and Doc fired back to hold her off and protect Tuna.

Sirens came from a distance. Cobra could hear them and was thinking what to do while still firing.

Tuna surprised DangPa from behind, hitting her hard on the side of the head. Blood ran from her temple as she went down, and in one swift movement Tuna snipped off her left pointer finger and put in his pocket. He stood up to see where Doc and 2Tall were when Cobra hit him with rounds from her FNAB-43. Tuna went down just as DangPa clawed her way up and reached Cobra's cover spot. Doc and 2Tall rushed over to Tuna while Cobra tossed two smoke grenades in their direction. They exploded.

When the smoke cleared, both women were gone.

Falcon had circled around the front to the edge of the beach and started running as fast as she could down the alley. Guns were now in her hands, and she wore only shorts and a half shirt that had been under the sarong. Dagger was also running for his life. He fired a couple of shots in the alley, doing anything he could to stay ahead of Falcon.

Falcon got herself up on a doorway step about one metre higher than the alley, and as Dagger ran by, she jumped right on top of him, wincing as her stitches pulled tight, straining to keep the skin together. They both went down. Falcon pulled herself up and stared into the barrel of his gun. He smiled. She held her breath. As his finger put pressure on the trigger, Doc came out of nowhere, punching Dagger a blow that almost killed him. He crumpled into a ball, the gun falling from his hand. Falcon let out a sigh and leaned forward. Doc came over and put a hand on her back, giving her a second. Together they pulled Dagger off the ground, knowing they needed to keep him alive for information. Sirens were getting closer.

"Thanks. I really didn't want to ruin another shirt," she said. Doc just laughed.

The Wookies did not want to be involved with the police. They left Berea's dead body, the armoured vans, and their passengers. Doc and Falcon grabbed Dagger, zip-tied his wrists, and gagged him. They fled to the car Tuna had prepared for their getaway. 2Tall arrived, virtually carrying Tuna. They piled into the vehicle and pulled onto the street.

"Let's go to the morgue," said Tuna. "My buddy there, Frank, will fix me up. And he can keep our boy here quiet until we figure out what to do with him."

They sped off, following their GPS to the morgue.

MONDAY, JUNE 1 | AFTERNOON | USA

"Sure it's okay we left him at the morgue?" asked 2Tall. He went over to the coffee pot on the counter in Falcon's room. "Anyone else want another cup?"

"I will," said Doc.

"Me too," said Falcon.

"I'm good," said Tuna.

"Are you?" asked Doc. "Really?"

"Yeah. Frank is one of the best. He can take out a bullet clean as a whistle, and his stitching is like a Ukrainian seamstress."

"Sure, on dead people," said 2Tall.

"Dead, breathing, the cleanup is still the same. I'm a little achy."

"He took out two bullets, Tuna," said Doc.

"Only two?" said Tuna.

"You wanted more?" asked Doc.

Tuna gave him a dirty look. "Well, I'm just going to lie on this bed for the rest of the day and you guys can bring me stuff." He smiled.

"Falcon, did you pop any stitches?" asked 2Tall.

"Almost, but I'm good. I put ice on it when I came into the room. It'll be okay."

"Back to my original question: is the guy we captured okay at the morgue?"

"For a while, yeah," said Tuna. "Frank has a holding room he can keep him in."

"Full of dead bodies?" asked Doc.

"Well, maybe he'll be grateful he's not one of them, and he'll happily talk."

"Maybe. Where's the finger you got off that other one who got away?" asked 2Tall.

"In a jar with formaldehyde. On the bathroom counter."

"Frank?"

"Yeah. He likes my finger collection. Was happy to help."

"All right. So, let's take stock here. We're all alive, maybe a little battered and bruised but okay. Agreed?" asked Doc.

They all nodded.

"There were four in that Cell. The two women got away, one without a finger," said Doc.

"Well, both are now missing a finger," said 2Tall.

"Right. And we know the other one is Sarah Thompson. With the finger Tuna snipped, we can figure out the other woman. One guy is dead, the other is sitting in a room with dead guys at the morgue, bound and muzzled."

"They didn't get the money," said Falcon.

"Correct," said Doc. "Do we know if any of the armoured van employees were killed?"

"Does it matter? Not to be harsh, but they are casualties here. We can't spend time on that," said Falcon.

"She's right," said Tuna. "It's the Cell that can give us info, and we have someone to question."

"Who will do that and when?" asked Doc.

"I'll do it," said Tuna. "You're all a bit squeamish in the morgue." He turned and looked at 2Tall, who kept sipping his coffee while analyzing the stucco design on the ceiling.

"Okay. What about Boss?" asked Doc.

"I've had word from him," said Falcon. "He's sent me an audio recording. Wants me to do voice rec on the voices. Once I figure out who they are, I'll put a track on their communications, and hopefully we'll start getting more puzzle pieces."

"And while you monitor that, I'll take Doc over to the morgue to question our boy. By this evening, we may have enough to pieces to complete the edge of the puzzle."

"Boss also said this Strike Force has put together a G8 golf tournament. He says the next G8 meeting is in France, so that's where the tournament will be held. He says he feels something is going to go down at that tournament. He wants us all to be there."

"When?" asked Doc.

"Wednesday. And he wants us all to be involved. I'm caddying, you'll be a caddy, 2Tall, Doc, and Tuna will be on audio surveillance, and Boss will be one of the pros."

"Wouldn't they have chosen all those people ages ago?" asked 2Tall.

"They certainly would have, but a few are going to get really sick in the next few hours," said Falcon.

"Well, you've got your work cut out for you. 2Tall, stay here, I don't want any of us alone right now. And with you here, Falcon doesn't have to watch her back as well as her computer screen."

"Got it," said 2Tall.

"Tuna?" He looked over at Doc. "That's enough lounging. Grab your finger in a jar; it might help loosen our boy's tongue. Let's go get some puzzle pieces."

CHAPTER SEVEN

THURSDAY, JUNE 4 | MORNING | FRANCE

Buckman checked out of his Paris hotel and drove to Guyancourt to do a little recon work before the Wookies arrived. He had a lot to do in a short amount of time: vet and book hotel rooms, scope out the course and routes in and out, purchase appropriate clothing, get a good meal. He figured he'd stay overnight there and drive back to Paris the next morning.

He had been pondering the information that Anderson had given him about who belonged to the voices in the recording he had sent to her. Something still didn't add up. He considered calling Kitch but realized he wouldn't have any new information. If they were going to get anything done at this tournament, they would need a bit more help. It would be swarming with security. He decided to call Mac. This was fast becoming her area of expertise, and he was going to need it. Plus, he was going to need weapons, surveillance equipment, surveillance earpieces, and rigs for the carts. This was turning into a full-scale mission. He'd buy what he needed now and figure out how to pay for it later. He and Mac had a lot of work to do. He dialled her number on the secure line.

THURSDAY, JUNE 4 | EVENING | BETWEEN COUNTRIES

Anderson was glad they had decided to fly business class. The seats had more leg room, and they were four abreast. They had much to discuss. Most of the other passengers in their cabin had switched off their lights, put on their sleeping eye masks, and were out. The cabin was quiet with the drone of the aircraft singing a soft lullaby. The Wookies still had their earpieces in, which meant they would be able to hear precisely what was being said using low, whispered voices. They hadn't wanted to discuss anything in the terminal, too many eyes and ears, real and cyber. It had been twenty-four hours of information overload. Anderson sipped a tea, Thornton and Foster a ginger ale, Harrod a Caesar with extra celery and a few olives.

"I love that you can actually recline these seats," said Harrod.

"I bet. You'd have your knees wrapped around your ears back there in steerage," said Foster.

Harrod sipped on his drink and smiled.

"Anderson? Any luck with Cole's voice recording?" asked Thornton.

"Oh, yeah. I already sent him the info. Get this. Those two voices? Security advisors from Canada and Britain."

"No shit," said Harrod, pulling his seat into a more

upright position. "Here we set out to look out for Kitch and stepped into a den of hyenas."

"Exactly. When I started to connect with their devices, I had to pull together bits and pieces and finally figured out that Buckman had been right; something is going down at this golf tournament."

"Well, Kitch said he heard five voices," said Thornton.

"So did Cole," said Anderson.

"Are they all security advisors?"

"Not sure."

"If they are, where are the other three from?"

"Well, we know one more: Italy," said Foster.

"How do we know that?" asked Anderson.

"Do you want to tell?" Foster looked to Thornton.

"Sure. When Foster and I got down to the morgue, our little friend was not happy about having been left with dead guys. He looked like he'd seen a ghost." He was waiting for laughter, but when all he got was blank stares, he rolled his eyes and continued. "We brought him some water, took off the muzzle. And before he could start with the silent treatment…." He handed it over to Foster.

"I put the finger jar on the table in front of him and told him it was from one of his team."

"He didn't seem to care too terribly," said Thornton. "Mercenaries are like that."

"But he cared a little bit more when I brought out my

pruners and said one of his fingers was going to join this one in the jar."

"Are there a few fingers in the jar now?" asked Harrod.

"Yes, but you're ruining the story," said Foster. "There's no rush; this is a long flight."

"I know, but I'd really like to get a little shuteye."

"Fine," said Foster. "Fill them in, Thornton."

"Apparently the hits this Cell were doing were for funding this Strike Force. But they never knew what for or where the messages came from or who the Strike Force was. Their money was transferred to their accounts, and that's all that mattered to them. True-blue mercenaries. Our boy was their computer geek, also good with a gun. When suddenly they were ordered to kill Ian, they were confused because initially they were hired to raid and rob. So our computer geek traced where the message came from and from whom."

"Who?" they all whispered in unison.

"The Italian security advisor."

"Fuuuck," again, in unison.

"Why did he want Ian out?" asked Harrod.

"Well, that our boy did not know."

"I'll find out," said Anderson. "I'm going through past communication from the other SAs; I'll add our Italian guy to the list. I'll have something by tomorrow afternoon."

"The G8: Italy, Canada, U.S., Britain, Japan, Russia, Germany, France. Correct?" asked Foster.

"Correct," they all answered.

"So if we assume that this Strike Force is a bunch of security advisors with a plot, that means the other two could be Japan, Russia, Germany, or France," said Foster.

"I'm going with Russia and Germany," said Harrod.

"Why?" asked Anderson.

"They're always looking for trouble."

"I wouldn't think France. They're more interested in quality cheese and wine," said Anderson.

"And Japan?" asked Thornton.

They all put their palms into the air.

"Maybe Frank can get a bit more out of our boy tomorrow," said Foster. "Leave him with the dead guys a bit longer and he may spill all his beans just to get out with the living again."

"Well, while the plot thickens," said Harrod, "I'm going to get some shut eye." As he was about to take out his earpiece while reaching for his sleep mask, Foster's voice blared into his ear.

"Jesus Christ," said Foster.

"What?" They all turned to face Foster.

"Frank just messaged me. Our boy figured a way out."

"Maybe the dead bodies gave him some tips," laughed Harrod.

"He escaped?" asked Thornton.

"He did," said Foster.

"Frank okay?" asked Anderson.

"Yeah, he was at home. Caught it on one of his monitors, someone racing out of the back door."

"How'd he get out?" asked Thornton.

"Frank is looking into that. Apparently his hands were zip-tied as he exited the building."

"Curious," said Anderson.

"Not really our concern now," said Foster.

"Good you took his finger," said Anderson.

"Two fingers, one from each hand," said Foster.

"Two fingers and the Italian guy," said Thornton. "Good info. Served his purpose."

"Anything else before I take out my earpiece?" asked Harrod.

"Get your beauty sleep, man," said Thornton.

They all reclined their seats; a little shuteye was something they could all use. Their next party started in about eight hours.

FRIDAY, JUNE 5 | MORNING | FRANCE

The prime minister of Canada put down his coffee and looked over at his security advisor.

"Seems risky. With all this bad press, it might be best to just bypass this summit and avoid the golf tournament. We don't need anything else to happen."

"I think that would be a mistake, sir. We have all the security needed in place. In fact, something like this may be just what is needed to regain confidence with voters."

"How on earth did this social media shitstorm get to this point?"

"Everything on the Internet seems to have a life of its own, and a very fast-paced life at that. It grew quickly, that's for sure."

"Are the other leaders attending?"

"As far as I know, no one has pulled out. So it would look very bad if we did."

"When do we leave?"

"Tonight, sir."

"Fine. Brief me on the way to the airport later."

The telephone rang, pulling the PM into another situation. The SA left the room. She made her way down the steps to an isolated outside courtyard where she pulled out her other phone and made a call, precisely at the arranged time. There were multiple people on the call.

"Is everyone's leader going to be in attendance at the summit?"

"Yes. It wasn't easy though. The agenda has definitely got under their skin."

"Good. It's all going like clockwork."

"Is everything in place for the tournament?"

"Yes, looks like Colin has lived up to his bidding."

"Has the Cell been made aware of their new assignment?"

"There are complications with that. Some members of the Cell have been compromised."

"Contact the other Cell. We need to take out the leaders' families at a moment's notice if there is any pushback."

"They have been notified and are refuelling."

"After this, we will be in charge."

"We'll meet again after the tournament at the safe house in Italy."

"Agreed."

The call ended.

FRIDAY, JUNE 5 | LATE MORNING | FRANCE

Buckman waited outside the Charles de Gaulle Airport in his Peugeot. It was a tight squeeze, fitting all those Wookies into the Peugeot, but the team made it work. He began the drive southwest of Paris and back to Guyancourt. He'd booked one room for each Wookie in four different hotels: Best Western, The Wish Versailles, Hotel Aerotel, and Ibis Budget Versailles Château Saint Cyr. In each room he had made sure the proper clothing for the tournament was laid out, appropriate to their undercover roles. Buckman was staying on-site at the Novotel Saint Quentin en Yvelines. They agreed to meet for dinner outside of Guyancourt at La Chalosse.

Anderson had garnered everyone a spot in the tournament and had filled them in on the details. She would be the caddy for the Canadian team. Buckman was the pro playing with the British team, Harrod the caddy for the Italian team. Thornton and Foster would keep tabs on the other teams. She explained that each team would have four people: the current leader of that country, their security advisor, a pro, and a caddy. The caddy would counsel the three players. The leader and SA would be in a cart, the pro and caddy would walk beside them. Order of play would be USA, Britain, Russia, Canada, Germany, Japan, Italy, and France. Thornton and Foster would be dressed as attendants at the club with access to all the equipment and rooms.

Buckman explained that they had to attend an orientation of sorts at the clubhouse at Le Golf National around 4:00 p.m. They all had security badges. While Buckman, Anderson, and Harrod were at the meeting, Thornton and Foster would check out the perimeter of the golf course and get a feel for the setting. Later that evening, they would meet for dinner outside of Guyancourt at La Chalosse to go over the plan.

Buckman dropped each of them off at their hotel so they could freshen up, grab a bite, and get changed. He said he would see them at the clubhouse, and Thornton and Foster could get a large private table at La Chalosse for 8:00 p.m.

"C.H.I.L.," Buckman said as he dropped each one off.

Buckman showed up at the golf course at 3:45 p.m. Anderson arrived at 4:00 p.m., Harrod at 4:15 p.m. It was an international gathering, and there were different languages bouncing around the room. The caddies were matched to their pro and then to the leader of one of the G8 countries. Buckman did some schmoozing with the other pros, talking shop and doing the appropriate shoulder pats while clinking half-full beer steins or something on the rocks.

Anderson had given Harrod some caddy lingo while

on the plane. He was a golfer, so he knew what he was doing, just needed a caddy prep. Anderson hobnobbed with the other caddies, having been at a number of tournaments in the past few years.

A few speeches were made. Nothing and no one looked overly suspicious. Security stayed within shoulder distance of their client or dignitary, hands behind the backs of their dark suits, occasionally talking into the mic on their wrist and putting a finger to their ear. Guards were posted at every door inside and outside, some in plain clothes, some in military uniform, some in police uniform. Being France, it would be kept pretty classy. All security would be carrying Glock 17s inside their suit or uniform jackets.

While the drinking and self-congratulating behaviour continued inside, outside Foster and Thornton were labelling the carts for each country and setting up the surveillance equipment.

Foster and Thornton left before the others. They went back to their hotels, changed, and made their way to La Chaloose.

The security advisors cautiously eyed each other from across the room. They were used to security and protection, although there was more at this event than usual. They knew they would not be able to converse with each other at all until after the event. They had laboured over every detail and were confident of the chain of events over the next few days. They watched as their leaders arranged for meetings with other leaders and bragged about their golf game. They were all invited to a dinner that evening, hosted by the French president within the golf clubhouse. Security was tight, and no one was allowed to leave without security clearance.

Alcohol and hors d'oeuvres were being served. The evening had begun.

———————

The Wookies entered the restaurant. Food and wine quickly filled their table.

"Now, this alone is worth coming for. What a spread," said Foster. He lifted his wine glass to his nose, sniffing with his eyes closed. He took a sip.

"You approve of my wine choice?" asked Buckman. Foster flashed a wider smile.

"Orgasm in a bottle," said Anderson. They all laughed.

"To orgasms," said Harrod, and they all lifted their glasses for a clink and a long sip.

"Anderson, any news?" asked Buckman.

"As a matter of fact," she said, "yes. Get this. I've been sifting through old communication from the Italian SA, and it turns out he changed his mind."

"About what?" asked Foster.

"About being involved?

"But he didn't pull out?" asked Thornton.

"No."

"Odd. Why change your mind but stay part of a group you now disagree with?" thought Harrod out loud.

"To still have impact on what they are doing," said Foster.

"Or to report back to someone else about what they are doing," said Buckman.

"Oh, that's better. I'm changing my answer to that," said Foster, taking another sip of wine.

"So he became a spy, a double-crosser," said Harrod.

"But why? This is something they are obviously invested in. What would make someone shift like that?" asked Anderson.

"Money," said Harrod.

"Leverage," said Buckman.

"Someone has something on him," said Anderson.

"Or has someone he knows," said Foster.

"Either way, Ian must have found out..." said Anderson.

"So he had to have him killed," said Harrod.

"And Kitch got in the way," said Buckman.

"But Kitch knew Ian, and they needed a replacement," said Anderson.

"We still don't know what this is all about, where this is all leading," said Harrod.

"What about our fingers," said Buckman, "anything come up?"

"I ran a trace on the fingerprints from my jars," said Foster. "Not a thing. They don't exist."

"Not really a surprise," said Harrod. "Mercenaries and rogue agents never want to get caught. They've removed their prints."

"Is that possible?" asked Thornton.

"Well, there's a genetic condition known as adermatoglyphia; these people have found a way to mimic that disease to their benefit, replicate the same skin type onto their hands. Voilà, no fingerprints," said Foster.

"Sounds painful," said Anderson.

"Not really. It's like a glove resembling skin. Ian used it too. That's why we couldn't get prints off him either," said Foster.

"Still sounds painful to me," said Harrod.

"Well, this wine is easing my pain," said Anderson. "Can we order another bottle?"

"One more, and then Perrier. We have a few big days

ahead, and long ones," said Buckman. "Carts set up?"

"Yup, all wired for sound," said Thornton. He'd been letting his beard grow back, but his hair was taking longer, so he opted for a wig and ball cap. He didn't want to take any chances of being recognized.

"Everyone have their earpieces?"

"Affirmative, Boss." They all smiled.

"Remember, this isn't a regular kind of tournament. Leaders don't have four days to give up; it's a short tournament, so we have tomorrow and Friday to get what we need. Who are the other countries involved, what is their agenda, what is the whisper smear campaign about?"

"Basically finding out what the fuck is going on," said Anderson.

"Basically, yeah. And remember, they still have Kitch in their sights." Everyone nodded. "We all clear?" Everyone nodded again. "Okay, let's order one more bottle of temptation."

"And some more of that cheese that's so creamy and succulent I could cry," said Foster. They all laughed.

"Don't cry, Foster; it isn't a good look," said Harrod.

The music playing was a mix of Gypsy Kings and Edith Piaf. Candles burned on each table beside a tall, thin glass vase with one single purple flower inside. Soft lights complimented the room, weathered red brick walls covered in vines surrounded the tables, and a large fountain softly babbled over rocks at the far end. Copies of Monet hung around the room, as well as some Margriet Hogue and Vahe Yeremyan.

"Oh my God, did you look at this menu?" asked Anderson. "I want a good look at some of this. And those aromas coming from the kitchen, OMG."

"Another orgasm?" asked Thornton.

Anderson completely ignored him. "I want the Confit de Canard with the Salade Niçoise, and the Chocolate Soufflé for dessert."

"And I think I will have the Boeuf Bourguignon."

"Me too," said Harrod.

"Yeah, that sounds about right," said Thornton. "And what beer do they have here?"

"Kronenbourg 1664," said Harrod. "I'll join you."

"Buckman?"

"*Coq au vin*, no question."

"Are we paying for this like we did at Fran's?" asked Foster.

"We still have no budget, Foster," said Buckman.

"Right," said Foster. "No dessert for you, Anderson."

"I'm paying for it myself, Dad."

"Now, now, kids. No fighting at the table," said Harrod.

"No, seriously, one tab. My treat tonight," said Buckman. "You all stepped up for my old man. I'm grateful. Plus, this may be the last meal we all have together."

"No way, I'll be back for another bottle of this red beauty here," said Foster.

They lifted their glasses and clinked, then looked for the waitress and ordered.

SATURDAY, JUNE 6 | FRANCE

Crowds and camera crews were everywhere as Dustin Johnson, the American golf pro, walked into the T box to execute the first drive of the tournament. It was a security nightmare. Buckman was glad he was playing and not on protection duty. The American president shook Johnson's hand and placed his ball on the tee. He was used to the flash of cameras and large crowds, security up his ass. He took his time, focused on the ball, and drove it down the fairway. The crowd cheered. He smiled and waved. His security advisor hit next. A good, solid drive. They then both proceeded to their cart while Johnson and his caddy waited at the side.

Britain was up next in the T box. Buckman approached, planted his tee into the earth, sized up his shot, and hit a tremendous drive, glancing over to Johnson with a wry smile. He had outdriven Dustin. The British PM took his shot, and Buckman gave him a high five as he stepped out of the T box. He was followed by his SA, one of three women on the course for the tournament. That was how it was organized; two countries would hit, and once they were finished the first hole, the next country would begin. Scores would be tabulated for that day, added to the score for the final day on Friday to determine the winner.

The carts scooted off, carrying the PM and SA, with Foster and Thornton situated near the course, tuned into all carts.

When Buckman's group got to the second tee, the American team was putting on the green. The second hole was a par 3, 210 yards. It had water in front all the way to the green. The British PM hit a great shot, making it to the front of the green. The spectators cheered. The SA set up her shot, but it landed in the water. She was visibly distressed. She wiped her brow and kept moving her hands down her thighs, like she was trying to smooth wrinkles from the fabric. Her eyes darted here and there, clearly not focused on her golf game. Buckman ended up in the trap behind the green. He chipped out of the trap and sank his ball for a birdie. Louder cheers.

At the end of nine holes, Buckman was three under par, the British PM at 44, his SA at 49. The leaderboard showed that as a team the Americans were in front, Britain a close second, France and Canada were tied, and the rest were trailing behind. The largest crowds were following the British and American teams.

Buckman knew the PM was an average golfer, but the SA played a lot and was normally really good but seemed preoccupied. As Buckman approached the tee on the tenth hole, he saw the Canadian team on the number nine fairway. Anderson and Buckman's buddy, the pro playing with the Canadian team, were laughing and joking as they walked along the fairway. *Anderson could use a little fun,* thought Buckman.

As Buckman flipped over to the eleventh green, he could see 2Tall with the Italian group. He seemed to be getting an earful from the Italian SA. Buckman couldn't tell if it was golf or gossip. Harrod saw him looking over and tossed a wave and a smile in his direction.

On the eleventh, Buckman hit a great shot, ringing the cup for almost a hole in one, but it ended up five centimetres from the hole. He tapped it in for an eagle. Buckman played well and ended up with a 66 at the end of the first day. The British PM gave him a pat on the back, marvelling at how he could put in a round like that, knowing he had another full-time job with his Secret Intelligence Service. Buckman just shrugged and gave his Buckman smile.

Buckman let the team go ahead to mark the scores. He wanted to watch for Anderson and Harrod.

Everyone had drinks on the terrace after the rounds were complete and then called it a night. Buckman was informed by his team that no new intel had been gathered. He was sure they hadn't made a mistake. Maybe it would all take place during the gala the next night. He was dead tired and couldn't wait to finally get a good night's sleep. Mac was arriving late the next afternoon, and he had another whole day of golf and surveillance.

Sunday proved to be a rigorous day of golf with teams moving up and down the leaderboard. As far as finding out more about the Strike Force, it had been relatively quiet. The Wookies were getting restless. They were beginning to wonder if they had misread the information. The gala was that evening. They had barely enough time to shower, change, and see what the evening would bring.

SUNDAY, JUNE 7 | EVENING | FRANCE

Anderson was in her hotel room preparing for the gala. Her dress was a dark blue satin gown, plunging at the back and the front, floor-length with a slit on one side that went mid-thigh. It was elegantly sexy. She swept her hair up onto the top of her head, and she wore long, slender silver earrings, matching the scalloped silver chain that wrapped around her neck and disappeared into her cleavage. On her feet were thin silver heels. She had a small black clutch purse that carried her lipstick and her gun, and she had a small knife fixed to her thigh, the one not exposed by the slit in her dress. She was ready. The guys said they would pick her up outside her hotel. She checked the time and headed for the door.

It had been a very successful tournament. Media coverage had been positive, and there had been no threats of protests. The golf had been stellar, and there had been some useful intel gathered from the carts. The Wookies had figured out one other crooked SA was from France, but the final one was still unknown. More was spoken between the US president and his SA out of the cart, so it remained a mystery. What Thornton and Foster had been able to piece together was that the SAs were threatening the leaders: follow our agenda or your family will pay. The exact nature of that agenda was still foggy. They hoped that would be cleared up during the gala. The Wookies had a revised plan.

Anderson stood in front of her hotel as a large black sedan pulled up beside her. A window rolled down, and hoots and whistles came sailing out. She smiled, a little embarrassed by the compliments but really happy it wasn't the Peugeot. She climbed into the front passenger seat. She turned and looked at Cole, all decked out in his tuxedo.

"My, my," she said, "don't you clean up nicely."

"Us?" said Thornton.

"No, you three are dressed like the help." Harrod and Foster raised an eyebrow to that comment.

"Fine, you guys clean up pretty nice in your security garb," said Anderson.

"Much better," said Foster, smiling like a Cheshire cat.

"Have you looked in a mirror?" Harrod asked Anderson.

"Yeah, you clean up pretty nicely yourself," said Foster.

"Woohooo!!" said Thornton.

"Okay, okay, let's get on with it," said Anderson, irritated that she was blushing.

Buckman laughed. "Okay, my beauties, back to work. Mac is on board, arrived a few hours ago. She's organized an interrogation room for us. She'll also be waiting for the word, and then she'll contact you, Thornton."

"I'll keep an eye for the opportunity to herd the Canadian SA to the restroom, where you can grab her, Anderson," said Harrod.

"I'll be ready to get the rest of the info we need out of her," said Foster.

"And I will be in the main gala room, keeping my watchful eye on the proceedings," said Buckman. "Everyone's earpiece online?" Nods around the sedan. "Weapons in place, if needed, which I hope will not be the case. For the rest of the night, we use our handles for any interactions. Can't be sure who will be listening. No point in compromising ourselves. Falcon, did you give your gun to Doc?"

"I did."

"We're all good," said Doc. "Let's get some bad guys."

Boss pulled up behind the clubhouse. Tuna and 2Tall exited the vehicle. Doc got into the driver's seat, and took Boss and Falcon around to the front entrance. They exited the vehicle, and Boss took Falcon's arm, walking her to the front door. Doc drove the vehicle to a hidden location. It was now his security intel centre.

"You really do look beautiful, Trish."

"Thanks, Boss. So do you." She winked at him.

At the front door, they went through security, then walked down the hall and into the dining room. The room usually filled with rectangular tables and chairs and walls full golf photos had been transformed into an event room: potted flowering plants, balloons and streamers, flags of all the G8 countries, colourful lights, round tables with white tablecloths, and a podium stage at the front of the room. The tables had seasonal, colourful flowers in thin vases and bottles of red and white French wines beside carafes of sparkling water. Other French dignitaries were invited to the gala dinner, increasing the number of tables and people in the room. Falcon was in the dining room as Boss's date that evening. The other three Wookies were masquerading as security detail and golf course staff. Boss and Falcon walked to their table. All the pros sat at the table of the leader they had played beside along with the security advisors.

Everyone settled into their seats and the doors closed as the French president moved to the podium to give the opening address. Security moved in front of each door. Staff came around, pouring wine into the goblets, since there would inevitably be a toast. More than one.

"Welcome, my friends and colleagues, to another successful gathering of the G8 countries," said the French president to a captive audience. A politician's favourite kind. "It is so important that we have events like these where we can get to know each other outside our places of business. We tend to solve problems differently when we are relaxed and enjoying ourselves. Even though our American friend ran away with the tournament cup this year, and the UK wasn't far behind, a good time was still had by all. Donations to the charity indicated prior to the tournament will be awarded to the first, second, and third-place teams. Before I announce the winners and their charities, please raise your glass and let us give a toast to continued unity amongst our nations as we work toward creating a better world for us all." Everyone lifted their glasses.

Boss slowed down the room and took out the noise. He surveyed all the tables, assessed where everyone was sitting, where the exits were, where the security guards were. So far, everything was calm. The speech ended and dinner was announced. While staff brought plates to the tables, a few leaders got up and went to speak with leaders at other tables. It was not uncommon at these events. Boss kept his eye keenly sharpened. He asked if anyone wanted a drink other than wine. Most were happy with their beverage, but Boss was hoping for a Jack on the rocks. He excused himself and made his way to the bar.

Falcon kept watch, casually talking with the wife of the British SA. Boss was halfway to the bar when the British PM walked by him, smiled, and slipped a piece of paper into his hand. He ordered his drink at the bar, and while he was waiting, he read the note in his hand. *Need to talk. My suite. 9 p.m. Just you.* Boss crumpled the note and put it in his pocket, taking his drink and heading back to the table.

The meal had been served; boeuf bourguignon, small onions, and tiny potatoes with spears of roasted asparagus, beautifully presented with intoxicating aromas. The culinary delights drew people back to their seats. There were ooohs and ahhhhs around the room as food found its way to tastebuds.

Boss felt his phone vibrate in his pocket. People were so engrossed in their food that they didn't notice him looking down at his phone. It was a text from Mac:

```
Canadian SA has just announced to her
staff that all intelligence projects
will have to be vetted through her.
Strange, not protocol. Just heard the
same is happening in Britain.
```

Boss exchanged a look of concern with Falcon and then quickly went back to idle chatter. He felt a shift in the room. An energy shift. He wasn't sure why, but something was different. He felt that prickle at the back of his neck. He knew it was time to act. He spoke the code words agreed upon to put the next part of the plan into action. They were all listening. "That is such a lovely necklace."

Falcon thanked him and said she had picked it up in France. Plan activated.

Falcon excused herself, showed her security badge to the guard, and went to the front desk to pick up the key Mac had arranged: the guest room where they would interrogate the Canadian SA. Tuna appeared in the lobby, looking like he was the next guest speaker, hair slicked back, black shoes, tailored slacks, white shirt, dark tie, black jacket. He was ready.

2Tall was still in the dining room, carrying a roll of wire for the sound system, since there was to be a dance later. He was dressed in a black golf shirt and black pants, like all the staff. He saw the Canadian SA leave her table and head for the doors, possibly the restroom. He signalled Falcon with a one-word text:

Move

The Canadian SA walked into the restroom and stood at the vanity, pulling a comb and lipstick from her clutch purse. Falcon came in and stood beside her, chatting and smiling, checking to see the restroom was empty. Tuna stood outside the door to ensure no one else entered.

As quick as a chameleon catching a fly, Falcon

reached out and grabbed the SA's arm, pushed her up against the wall, and made it clear they were going to take a quiet walk. Falcon smiled and asked if she understood, twisting her arm until she winced to make her point.

The SA was startled, shaken.

Falcon pulled her dress to one side, revealing her knife. "Don't force my hand," she said.

The SA swallowed hard and nodded.

They walked out together, like two gal pals, and Tuna fell in step behind them. The SA was stone-faced but didn't sound an alarm. Falcon unlocked the guest door and took the woman inside, pushing her into a chair and taking her clutch purse. Falcon then moved to stand beside the door as Tuna made his grand entrance. For an old retired CSI cop like Tuna, this kind of interview was his bread and butter. He was practically salivating. He pulled up a chair and sat opposite the SA, their knees touching.

"I demand you release me. This is outrageous treatment," she said.

"Oh, I've only just begun," Tuna crooned. He didn't like them cocky. He pulled his finger jar out of his pocket and held it up in front of her face. She started to gag and move away. Foster grabbed her hair and pulled her closer to the jar. "There's only three little piggies in here. I think we need a fourth." He smiled. He thought she was going to vomit on his shoes. It didn't take long after that for

Tuna to get all that he wanted out of her. Boss heard it all in his earpiece.

"How long are you going to keep me here?" she asked.

"I'll let you know."

The dinner was finishing up, and awards and jokes had been dished out. The dance would begin soon. Boss knew he needed to get himself back to the hotel to meet the PM. He assumed it would be quick and they would be back before anyone noticed they were gone. He sent a text to Tuna:

Sit with Canadian SA.

Once through security, Boss knocked on the door of the PM's room in the building adjacent to the clubhouse. The PM opened the door and stood back for Boss to enter. He was visibly shaken and offered Boss a Scotch. Cole declined, but the PM poured one for himself and took a long drink.

"You've got me out of a lot of jams in the past, Mr. Buckman. This one is a doozy. Out on the golf course today…"

"Your SA threatened your life and that of your family if you didn't comply."

"How did you know?"

"Well, that is my job. It's a long story, but the pieces have finally all come together. Your job and your family have been threatened if you don't comply, correct?"

"Yes. Apparently, this whole smear campaign is their doing. They want to take over with this Strike Force, as they call themselves. Not this election, but the next one. This time, they want to govern through me. I become their puppet, or…."

"Yes. I know. My team has a plan. How fast can you get five leaders into this room?"

"Which ones?"

"Canada, US, France, Italy. And tell them to be quick. We need to get back to the dining room before anyone really notices."

The PM turned and picked up a phone. "They'll be here in minutes. The tables are being cleared away for the dance. Everyone is taking a break."

While they waited, the PM called his wife to make sure she was safe. He gave her a coded warning, which meant she should leave and go to the safe house with the children. Boss checked in with Mac, telling her he was meeting with the five leaders in ten minutes. Mac clicked into gear, having worked with the G8 Security Intelligence Service in the past, part of a joint task force. She pulled out operations plans from past G8 summits and began looking for counterparts in each country. She would then make the calls to each one, and they would implement surveillance for the families of their leaders. It would become an international liaison between the five countries.

The leaders began trickling into the room. When all five were present, Boss and the British PM asked if they had received the same threats during the golf tournament from their SA. They all looked wide-eyed at each other in agreement. Buckman said his team was on it. He needed the code word from each of them in order to initiate a countermove so that their families could be taken into safety. And his team would then start dismantling the whisper campaign. Each leader wrote down their codes on pieces of paper. Buckman conveyed them to Mac through a secure network and then burned the papers. He told them all to quickly go back to the gala and act as if nothing out of the ordinary was happening.

Boss made his way back to where Tuna had the Canadian SA. He walked in, owning the room, and stood above the SA. Tuna got up and stood beside Falcon.

"Did you know you had a dissenter?"

"What? How do you know that?"

"The how isn't important. Right now you are in a lot of trouble."

"That can't be true; he would never betray us. We began all of this to get China under control. It was the only way to bring our five countries together. As a start.

To not be swayed by China's shiny toys, manipulations, military might at the expense of every citizen around the globe. It is a noble plan. Antony wouldn't betray us like that."

"Well, he did. Remember in the late 1800s the prophetic words of Sir John Dalberg-Acton, 8th Baronet… 'Power tends to corrupt, and absolute power corrupts absolutely.' You were playing with fire. Nothing is noble when mercenaries are involved and people are killed. Your Italian friend secretly ordered Ian to be killed because he caught wind of his plan and wanted out. Ian was going to tell the British PM at the environmental summit in Toronto all about the Strike Force. And Antony could not let that happen. He was to be killed there. But I got in the way. And then my father almost died too when the plan had to be altered."

"Kitch. Yes. That was awful. None of us really knew what went wrong. But Antony wouldn't betray us—he just wouldn't."

At that moment, the door opened and 2Tall pushed the Italian SA into the room and into a chair opposite the Canadian SA. "Ask him yourself before you are both taken into custody."

Antony sat in the chair, a broken man.

"Why, why Antony? It was foolproof. It was working. Why?"

"Because they have my sister."

"Who?"

"The Chinese government." Everyone in the room froze, only eyes moving. No one was breathing.

Boss spoke first. "What do you mean? Explain."

"Somehow they found out what we were planning. I mean, it is exactly why we started all this in the first place. And then it was all happening to me. Their surveillance is without parallel. If you think any government does anything without China knowing, you are crazy. We wanted to try to stop their march to global rule. It would at least have been a beginning. We tried talking to our leaders, but they weren't interested in hearing anything. So we created our own Force. And China found out. Instead of stopping us, they wanted to let things run and eventually take over instead of us. A faster route to international rule, I guess. First, they offered me money, but I declined. Then I heard my sister, who was working over there, was taken into military custody. You know what that means."

"Seriously, you should have told us."

"What would you have done?"

"Encouraged you to let her go. You scarified the wrong person; you sacrificed Ian."

"You're telling me I should have let them torture my sister to death?"

"Antony, they will do it anyway. At least we would have gained a small foothold."

Antony began to cry, head in his hands.

The Canadian SA dropped her arms to her sides, a sign of giving up. The strap of her dress slipped off her shoulder, and Boss noticed the tattoo.

"What is that?" he asked.

"Vanity in the end. We saw ourselves as the knights of the new round table. The sword coming up was in protest to current policy. A Strike Force for justice."

"From what I know about Ian, that's why he agreed to work with you. He saw himself as a Robin of Sherwood, my dad said."

"Yes, that's true."

"And when things started going sideways…"

"He couldn't be part of it anymore, and Antony had him killed." She put her head into her hands. Her shoulders starting to shake as she cried.

"Contact your other members. Let them know what Antony did to Ian. That it was because of that your whole operation has crumbled in on itself. And then tell them their intelligence orders have been reversed, and we are putting protections on all the families of the leaders. It may be *your* families you should be concerned about now."

Boss turned and walked out of the room, nodding to

Falcon and Tuna to follow. 2Tall fell in behind them. They left them there alone, sitting in their chairs with the tattoos inked on their shoulders.

LATE JUNE | CANADA

The Wookies shared a drink on *Windy Girl.* It was a warm day on the water. Summer winds were just around the corner. It had been a crazy seventy-two hours.

Anderson had been busy putting an end to all whisper campaigns and destroying the database. Thornton had been working with Mac and the international intelligence community to make sure all five leaders' families were safe, and the leaders themselves. They were in the process of neutralizing all mercenary cells working for the Strike Force. They had the blessing of each leader and their intelligence forces. It had been a wake-up call for everyone. Some of the leaders had vowed to take a stronger stance on China and change some of their policies. They were looking at the next election with very different eyes.

Kitch climbed on board the *Windy Girl*, carrying a twelve-pack. Everyone was on deck, enjoying the sun and warm breezes. It was time to heal. Kitch handed the cold beer around, and everyone popped a can. They lifted them up and held them all together in the air.

"To Ian," said Kitch.

"To Ian," they all repeated.

They drank heartily, jostling and joking with each other. Cole's phone vibrated in his pocket. He looked at the text and then at his Wookies. Everyone paused and looked back at Cole.

"Wanna stay out of retirement?" he asked.

SEPTEMBER | FIVE G8 COUNTRIES

The Canadian Security Advisor received an appointment to an overseas diplomatic post outside Afghanistan, no return date formalized.

The American security advisor was assigned to Alaska to a government desk job. His ranch was in the hands of employees for the time being.

The British security advisor went to a Middle East post and died in a car crash.

France reassigned their security advisor to an army post working in a military jail as a guard.

The Italian security advisor died of unknown causes. His sister was never heard from again.

The duties of security advisors were altered in all countries, making them more accountable and less autonomous.

China remains a threat.

ACKNOWLEDGEMENTS

DON HAWKINS:

A special thanks to our friends and colleagues in the Security and Intelligence World of Law Enforcement and Military Operations. Your bravery and courage in past and present assignments keeps us all safe.

I would also like to thank Marina for encouraging me to reach out into the world of Security Intelligence and develop our story. Over many cups of coffee and beers (not at the same time) Marina worked with me to create the cast of characters that make up our story and guided me as the story developed. Then she took the story line and the cast and made it come to life with the magic of her written words. Thanks, Marina, for making this dream come true for me.

MARINA L. REED:

I'd like to thank all of the people who consulted with me on this story, making sure all the military details and intricate manoeuvres were accurate. I am not allowed to use many of your names for your own protection, but you all know who you are. Thank you for helping me develop a tough, edgy side. I can thank Matthew Ysinga by name for his firearms expertise. Matt was there at the other end of the computer or cellphone line to answer my questions and educate me about the kaleidoscope of the weapons landscape. I could not have done it without you.

Thanks to our editor, Allister Thompson, who always gives the straight goods and helps make sure the book is the best it can be. To Alanna Rusnak and Chicken House Press for making *On the Edge* available for everyone to read and enjoy. Alanna, you are a joy to work with. To J. Mitchel Reed for his vision and creative talent in designing the cover. Your art really does say a thousand words. To Mark Marquis who helped me create *Windy Girl.*

And last but certainly not least, to Don who allowed me to be part of his dream and taught me how intricate and multilayered the world of Security Intelligence really is. We owe a lot to those who protect us. Thanks Don, for having a great story, for being a wonderful colleague, and always having a pint of pilsner ready and waiting.

ABOUT THE AUTHOR/CREATORS

Marina has lived and worked around the world as a journalist, educator and artist. She is the author of ten books, freelance articles, online workshops and television current affairs programs. She believes in the empowerment of individuals. Marina is currently working on her next novel. Follow her at MarinaLReed.com

Don served for over 30 years with a large Canadian Police Service, coming in direct contact with many homicide investigations. As a Detective Staff Sergeant, he specialized in International Security Operations. He is currently based in Toronto where he owns and operates a Security Consulting Firm.

Look for the new Cole Buckman novel,
Shadow Man, coming soon from Chicken House Press.

Subscribe to Marina's newsletter by going to her website.
Book her to speak at your book club gathering or event.
Send her your thoughts and comments.
Go to MarinaLReed.com